DIVE BAR DETECTIVE

An "Olive or Twist" Mystery
Book One

by
Archer Hay

Ah-ha! Publications
Milwaukee, Wisconsin

Cheers! [signature] "Archer Hay"

Ah-ha! Publications
Milwaukee, Wisconsin
https://www.archerhay.com

Please send all permission requests to:

kelly@archerhay.com
or
jim@archerhay.com

TABLE OF CONTENTS

CHAPTER ONE

"I'm starting to get worried. It's been more than twenty-four hours," Brandy said into the phone. She didn't announce herself. She gave no context. She didn't have to. This call was the continuation of a saga that had been unfolding over the past day and a half.

"Well, do you think we should go over there?" Emily said on the other end. "What do you want to do? Say the word. It's up to you."

Emily and Brandy had been best friends since high school, going on twenty-five years. Emily would help Brandy day or night, no questions asked. If Brandy had a body to bury, Emily would show up with garbage bags and a shovel. Emily had answered half-a-dozen similar calls from Brandy over the last day or so. Each time, she tried to gently lead Brandy to the unwelcome truth, but Brandy was still fixated on the likelihood something was wrong—not morally wrong, but terribly wrong.

So, Emily tried to be supportive without sounding cynical.

"Twenty-four hours isn't *that* long to go without a text or a call. It's already almost 11 p.m. He's probably sleeping. Give it 'til morning," Emily advised.

"But I've watched enough Dateline to know that when your gut is telling you something's wrong you need to listen and act fast."

"This isn't a 'Dateline' situation. I think it's more of a 'To Catch a Cheater' situation. I know you don't want to hear that, but . . ."

Brandy was dismissive and insisted on adhering to her own theory. She counted and re-counted the hours as she rambled about how many failed attempts she had made to reach Eric—giving painfully specific commentary about why each subsequent unanswered text or call justified a higher level of concern.

"Hey! Hey, listen to me," Emily said, trying to focus Brandy's attention. "I know it's not like him. I know he's never done this before. I know what you're thinking. You're imagining the worst. I know, I know, I know. But what do you want to *do* about it? Telling me you're worried doesn't do any good."

There was a pregnant pause on the other end of the phone.

"Then let's go," Brandy said. "And I'm calling Danny and Caroline."

"Why?"

"So, they can drive. I'm too worked up. And I'm scared to death of what I'm going to find."

"And you don't want your car anywhere near there?"

"Exactly," Brandy said, sounding more confident.

"Then let's do this!" Emily said.

It was close to midnight when Brandy, Emily, Danny, and his fiancé, Caroline, rolled quietly into Eric's neighborhood with their headlights off. They parked half a block down the street and sat quietly in the car while Brandy continued to call and text Eric incessantly.

The street was quiet, and a dim blue light glowed in Eric's second-floor apartment. They fixed their eyes on the shadows. Did something cause the light to flicker? Did something move in the front window? His gold Monte Carlo was in the driveway with an unfamiliar red Toyota Civic parked behind it. Brandy wasn't sure if seeing his car there was a comfort or a concern.

"Have you tried tracking his location?" Caroline asked.

"No," Brandy said dismissively. "I don't need to do that. I trust him. We've been together for two years."

"Well, you should track him. Can't hurt. Every phone comes with some kind of 'friend finder' app. If he won't let you follow him, he's cheating on you. Plain and simple."

"That's not necessarily true," Brandy protested. Then expecting to make a point, she said, "Are you tracking Danny?"

Danny shifted in the front seat and turned around to face Brandy and Emily in the back.

"I'll take that one," he said raising a finger in the air. "She burst into the jewelry store as I was buying her engagement ring shouting 'Ah ha! I caught you. What are you buying her? Who is she?'"

"Danny's perfectly fine with it, aren't you, Danny?" Caroline said.

"Of course. I'm completely fine with it," he said, sounding sincere.

"Good boy," Caroline said as everyone chuckled.

"I don't think you need to even bother with a locator," Emily said. "That's not your red car in the driveway. Case closed."

Brandy was firm that her concern was based on nothing more than a genuine fear Eric had been murdered in his apartment.

He lived above his shop where he built and modified custom motorcycles. He dealt with some questionable clients—the kind who liked to use nicknames and pay cash; the kind who couldn't pick-up their bikes until they got out of jail. Maybe it was a robbery gone wrong? Or an organized hit? Brandy's mind raced and scanned for the most likely explanation—never pausing at the possibility he was ghosting her.

The shop was dark. There were bikes in varying stages of completion inside the locked fence that surrounded the perimeter of the property. If Brandy could get to the front entrance of the shop, she could pound furiously on Eric's front door which was adjacent to the shop entrance. He wouldn't likely hear her any other way.

Desperate for a sign that he was ok, but also afraid to confront her deepest fears, she continued to stare at the lights and shadows in the apartment.

"I'm going to jump the fence," she announced abruptly.

"I'm going with you," Emily said.

Danny and Caroline also immediately followed suit as they all sprung from the car.

Brandy was on a mission now. There was no turning back. She was either going to be a hero or a witness. She climbed over the chain link fence while the others stayed on the street. She pounded on the door.

"Eric!" she yelled. "Eric! I know you're in there. Your car's here and your lights are on. Just give us a sign that you're ok!" She laid her right ear flat against the heavy door.

There was no response. No flutter of the curtains, no flicker of light, no shadow of movement.

After ten minutes of yelling and pounding, Brandy heard a loud whisper from above her.

"Hey!" It was Caroline. "Look what I found!" She was sitting in the crook of a "V" that attached a small wooden porch on the second level to the brick wall below. She tried to stand up and reached for the slats of the railing around the porch. Grabbing hold, she awkwardly pulled herself up.

"What are you doing?" Danny whispered.

"I'm going in this other door!" she whispered back.

As Caroline climbed over the porch railing and righted herself, she followed Brandy's lead and pounded on the door.

"Eric! It's Caroline. Brandy's here. She's worried about you. Answer the door!"

Again, there was no response.

Caroline cupped her hands around her eyes and peered through the window in the door. She tugged on the locked door in frustration.

Woop. Woop. Two staccato blips announced the police cruiser that had pulled up to the scene.

Caroline was now trapped on the small landing. A police officer approached Brandy, Emily, and Danny.

"Is there a problem here, folks?"

"Thank God," Brandy said. She launched into a soliloquy about how they had reason to believe their friend was in that apartment, but they hadn't heard from him in over twenty-four hours despite multiple calls and texts. It wasn't like him to be so unresponsive and they were concerned for his welfare.

"And what's she doing up there?" the officer asked, shining a flashlight up at Caroline.

Caroline gave him a sheepish wave.

"I think I'm stuck up here," she said. "He didn't answer the front door, so I got up here to see if we could get in through the porch door, but it's locked."

Brandy cited Eric's car in the driveway and the dim glow of lights in the apartment as evidence he was likely inside, which made his refusal to open the door all the more ominous.

The officer agreed. He returned to his car and almost before he had walked back to reconvene with the group, four more police cruisers arrived—along with a fire truck.

One of the officers took Brandy aside to review evidence of her mounting concern and proof of prior occasions when calls and texts to Eric were answered quickly. Another officer pounded on the front door of the apartment, yelling to Eric much as Brandy did, and peeking in the shop windows. A third police officer called the utility companies to try to find out if Eric, in fact, lived in the residence and who owned the property.

Believing they might just knock and leave, Emily pulled one of the officers aside and added, "I believe he may be diabetic, too. Write that down." She put on a pair of reading glasses to make sure he complied.

Meanwhile, the firetruck backed up to the mini-deck off the side of the second floor where Caroline was waiting in embarrassment to be rescued. But after assisting her down the angled ladder, they were surprised to see a fireman going back up the ladder with an ax in his hand.

"What is he doing?" Brandy asked one of the police officers.

"We're executing a welfare check. You said he hasn't been seen or heard from for more than twenty-four hours and his car is in the driveway and lights are on in the apartment. No one is answering our calls or our orders to open the door. Our supervisor has approved a medical emergency break-in. So, we can't leave until we make contact. We're going to break the door down and see if he's in there."

"Oh my!" Brandy gasped. Had she overreacted? Did she let things spiral out of control? Maybe she should have listened to Emily and given him until morning.

In addition to being a bike mechanic, Eric was a woodworker. He had designed and built that upstairs patio door himself. It pained Brandy to see it splinter and scar as the fireman chopped at it.

Finally, he broke through and went inside. Everyone waited anxiously. Policemen spoke in numbers quietly over their shoulder radios. Firemen milled around below the patio deck. After about two minutes—which felt like two hours—the fireman came out the same door Brandy had been banging on earlier.

"Ma'am," he said. Brandy knew it wasn't good if she was being called "ma'am." "We found two people. A man and a woman. Can you come upstairs and tell me if it's your friend."

Brandy's heart started pounding as rage bubbled up and seared her throat like a shot of Fireball. She took the stairs from the front door to the upper apartment two at a time with her long blonde ponytail whipping behind her.

"Eric!! You lowlife scumbag!" Brandy screeched as she careened around the corner into the living room. Two empty—but dirty—wine glasses were on the coffee table. Two bottles of wine and several beer cans surrounded them.

"I can't believe you cheated on me!" Brandy screamed as she marched to the bedroom. There, she saw two bodies—a man and a woman—tangled in bedsheets, mouths gaping, with their eyes shut.

"I hope you're happy now! This is what you get when you don't answer my calls or texts for two days. Wake up!" she yelled as she shook the edge of the mattress. "Look at me!"

The man groaned and made an uncoordinated effort to turn away and cover himself with the sheet. The woman's eyes fluttered from Brandy's bed-shaking and from Eric's movement shifting the bed.

"I think I'm going to puke," the woman said.

"You can have him, you skank!" Brandy ran from the bedroom, unaware that tears were welling in her eyes. Emily and the fireman had made it as far as the living room. Upon seeing Emily, Brandy burst into tears.

"Is that him, ma'am?" the fireman asked.

Brandy couldn't speak. She nodded her head 'yes' and wilted into Emily's waiting embrace.

"He's in there passed out with some 20-year-old super-skank," Brandy said between muffled sobs.

"Shhh," Emily said as she hugged Brandy. "It's ok." She spun Brandy around and, keeping hold of her shoulder, started grabbing items from the living room.

"What are you doing?" Brandy asked.

"I'm grabbing your stuff. He's not keeping it all. Over my dead body!"

They were in full looter-mode when a handsome police officer came out of the bedroom.

"Ma'am, your property is a civil issue, so I'm not going to stop you from gathering your personal belongings. But I'm not going to stand here all night while you reminisce. You've got two minutes to get what's yours and get downstairs."

The officer stood watch as Emily worked-over the living room and kitchen. Meanwhile, Brandy detoured to the bedroom and gave a hard hammer fist to Eric's Bojangles. Still very inebriated, he only moaned and made a weak attempt to move his arms.

"Alright. You're done here," the officer said to Brandy. "That's domestic violence. You can't assault the man." He gently steered her back to the hallway.

"Am I going to jail?" Brandy asked through red, puffy, puppy-dog eyes.

The cop looked at her with pity. "Not if you two get out of here and get downstairs right now."

Emily collected Brandy and handed her some odds and ends to help carry. The police officer's glare directed them down the stairs and outside.

"Look at the bright side," Emily said. "You destroyed his artisan door. And maybe she's not a super-skank? Maybe she's just your everyday garden variety slut?"

As they walked past the gold Monte Carlo and red Toyota, Emily nonchalantly keyed both cars, leaving long hideous scars along the passenger sides of both vehicles.

"Why did you do that?" Brandy asked.

"Because I knew you wouldn't," Emily said with a wink.

They rode mostly in silence on the way back to Brandy's house to drop her off. Caroline kept trying to apologize—saying if she hadn't climbed up on the balcony and looked like a burglar, the cop would have had no reason to stop.

It all went in one ear and out the other.

Brandy spoke mostly to herself, or to no one in particular, as she marveled at what her life had become and tried to give herself a pep talk.

"I'm forty frickin' years old and single again. *Again*." The word landed heavy on her and unleashed an avalanche of tears. "I'm a has-been paralegal. Never been married, never had kids. I'm just a bartender. All my friends are drunks or on probation or the same people I hung out with in high school—no offense. There's been NO forward motion in my life. Zilch."

"Wow, you really know how to sell yourself," Emily said sarcastically. "And even though you're forty, you don't look a day over forty-seven." Brandy gave a weak grin and punched Emily in the arm—more for making her smile when she wanted to be mad, but also in acknowledgement of a first-rate insult.

"Stop feeling sorry for yourself. He didn't want you. End of story. Who cares?" Emily said. "How can you be sad about losing a guy who clearly isn't interested anymore? Sayonara! I say it's a blessing."

Proving she heard not a word of Emily's sermon, Brandy yelped. "Oh! I almost forgot! Take me to my sister's, not to my house. She's watching Hairy for me." She sunk in defeat into the back seat as she added, "And I really don't feel like being by myself tonight."

Hairy Pawter was Brandy's big, hairy, slobbery mixed breed dog. He was the main boy in her life and she almost felt bad that he wasn't enough—that she still wanted to be loved and admired by a human. If she could find a man who loved her and looked at her the way Hairy did, she'd be set for life!

"We'll chauffeur you to wherever you want to go, m'lady," Caroline said.

Caroline and Danny, who were engaged to be married and who had become two of Brandy and Emily's closest friends, sat awkwardly in the front seat—hyperaware of their happy coupledom, college educations, and generally trouble-free life. They felt nothing but guilt at having been co-conspirators on a night that put a glaring exclamation point on all the things they had that Brandy didn't.

Their relationship wasn't all sweetness and light, though. As if Brandy's ordeal had belonged to Caroline, she snapped at Danny. "If you *ever* turn your locator off, well . . . let me put it this way . . . no one will *ever* find you."

"Jeez. I won't." He rolled his eyes at her hyperbole. Or what he hoped was hyperbole.

Soon, they pulled up in front of Ginny's house. Brandy had called ahead to tell her sister to leave the door unlocked and to let her know she was going to crash on her couch.

As Brandy gave a half-assed effort at getting ready for bed, her feelings of humiliation at making a public scene gave way to a feeling of superiority. Her initial instinct was to tell no one what had happened—it made her look needy and insecure at best and conniving at worst. But as the night turned to dawn, she had managed to convince herself she had acted not only reasonably but honorably. She had nothing to be ashamed of.

And after coming to that conclusion, she could not wait to go to work and tell all the regulars at "Olive or Twist" that she had to call the fire department to break down Eric's precious artisan door only to find him passed out with a super-skank.

CHAPTER TWO

The next morning, Hairy licked Brandy awake as if he knew she needed some extra kisses.

"So, rough night, I take it?" Ginny said.

Brandy mumbled and wiped her mouth as she tried to wake up.

"Well, I had a pretty rough night, myself," Ginny continued. "You forgot to bring Hairy's squeaky pickle."

"Oh no!" Brandy groaned, realizing immediately what that meant.

"He cried for an hour straight."

"I'm sorry," Brandy whined. "I got ready in such a hurry. And obviously, my mind was elsewhere."

"It's no big deal. He finally calmed down when I turned on some quilting videos on YouTube. He sat right next to me and watched the whole time."

Ginny was fourteen years younger than Brandy but going on sixty. Ginny was a . . . ahem . . . , "bonus baby" that came along after Brandy and her older brother were mostly raised. So, Ginny grew up almost like an only child. Despite their age difference and the fact Brandy was the much older sister, Ginny was the much older soul. She liked to scold and give advice almost as much as she liked canning and water aerobics.

"Well, next time you have to go on a midnight mission to save a boyfriend who doesn't need saving, you should take a minute to get yourself together. For Hairy's sake."

"Whatever you say, Boss. What time is it?" Brandy asked, still lying on the couch stroking Hairy's head.

"It's almost 11:00 a.m."

Brandy sprung to her feet with ninja-fast reflexes. "Oh crap! I'm supposed to work at 11:00 a.m."

"Then you have about six minutes."

"Can you drive me? I got dropped off last night. My car's at my place."

"Yes, but you're going to be a few minutes late. I'm boiling eggs and I can't let them sit in the water too long."

"Did you feed Hairy?"

"Of course. We ate and we played, didn't we Hairy?" Ginny said in an excited voice that made Hairy's tail wag.

Brandy washed her face to rid herself of the raccoon eyes she had after last night's cry-fest ruined her mascara.

"Do you have a clean shirt I can borrow? Mine smells like washed-up potential and bad decisions!" she yelled, already staring into Ginny's perfectly organized closet.

"Sure. But you have to return it clean. Not just folded. But clean."

"Do you have anything that doesn't scream 'Sister Wife?'" Brandy asked.

"Just because I dress modest or conservative doesn't mean I'm some kind of evangelical prude."

"Funny, because I was just going to ask if you were going for 'Amish-chic.'"

Ginny shot her a "ha ha, very funny" glare from the doorway.

"Nope. Nope. Amish. Amish. Handmaid's Tale. Nope," Brandy said as she fashion-policed each shirt in turn.

Finally, she pulled a silky camisole from the back of the closet. Ginny immediately snatched it from her hands and blushed.

"You can't wear that! It's a slip. It's like a bra!"

"I'm wearing it. On the outside. And so should you, Julie Andrews."

To emphasize her point, and to tease Ginny, Brandy playfully stripped off her t-shirt right in front of her. Ginny politely turned around. "Hey, if ya ain't seen a set of perky double D's by now . . ."

"You have more going for you than your breasts. You realize that, don't you?" Ginny said in a motherly tone, still facing away.

"You're no fun," Brandy said smoothing her staticky hair into a ponytail. "Let's go. Come on, Hairy!" she yelled.

*   *   *

Ginny pulled her Hyundai Sonata up to the side door of "Olive or Twist." Brandy rolled out of the passenger side and let Hairy out of the back. She then poked her head back through the passenger side window and said, "Can you bring me dinner?" in a baby voice to Ginny.

"I can't. I have four piano students today. All from 3:30 p.m. to 5:30 p.m."

"Then come at 5:30 p.m. when you're done," Brandy said. "Bring me anything. I'm not picky."

"Five thirty is a little late to be eating dinner don't you think?"

Brandy squinted in disbelief.

"Never mind," she said as she rolled her eyes and called Hairy who was sniffing the flower beds along the side of the bar.

As soon as she entered the bar with Hairy, Brandy threw her hands in the air and yelled, "Mama's home! Hold your applause!"

Several old men sitting at the bar turned to look. A couple of them gave some encouraging "whoops!" A middle-aged husband and wife—lunchtime regulars—sat at a bar table by the window and gave Brandy a smile and a wave.

"Hi, Chaz," Brandy said to her boss. Luckily, it was the first Friday of the month—Chaz's one and only obligatory check-in on his corner bar. He didn't care that she was a few minutes late. He didn't care that she brought her dog to work as her "bouncer." He didn't care about much of anything as long as the bar kept funneling profits into the trust fund that owned it on his behalf until he could turn 30 and own it in his own name.

"Thanks for holding down the fort until I could get here," Brandy said. "I'd have had a line outside if it wasn't your Friday. So, I'm glad you were here to let everybody in."

"It's cool. No worries," Chaz said. "Alright," he said, giving the place a superficial once-over. "You all good here? Can I go?"

"Yeah, we're good. See you next month."

Chaz left out the side door.

When he was out of earshot, Brandy sarcastically said, "Oh no. Don't worry, Chaz. I'll get everything turned on. Oh no. It's no trouble at all."

Chaz had let people into the bar when it opened at 11:00 a.m., but that was all he did. He hadn't put the cash in the drawer or even turned on the lights.

"He don't do much, does he?" asked one of the old men, trying to commiserate with her plight.

"Not really. I guess that's one of the perks of being the boss. Did he even get you a drink, Brownout?"

All the regulars at "Olive or Twist" had endearing nicknames and signature drinks. Brownout's real name was Gary Brown, but he didn't know when to quit—so after an epic night of drinking his "usual" (a triple rail vodka in a pint glass with extra ice) the next morning was always a "Brownout."

"Naw. Not yet," he said. "But I got time. You go ahead and take care of your business. I got nowhere to be."

The other patrons generously agreed to be patient while Brandy opened up. In gratitude, she tried to race through her usual morning checklist in double-time.

The bar was a small single-level brick building on the corner of 76th and Adler in the village of West Allis—a small blue-collar suburb on the fringe of Milwaukee, Wisconsin proudly considered one of America's drunkest cities.

She flipped off the small electric sign above the front door with the bar name: "Olive or Twist." No need to waste an expensive fluorescent bulb when the light of the noon sun would suffice. Besides, those bulbs were a pain to change. She also dusted off the slatted bench outside under the front windows where patrons could wait for the bus that stopped several times each day on the corner. Brandy, a talented and avid gardener, had taken the initiative to lovingly plant annuals around the perimeter of the building—to make it more bright and inviting. Customers loved her gardening—raving it was sheer artistry. So, she made certain to water the flower beds she had cultivated.

The bar's interior was dark and stuffy. The ceiling was low, the wood was dark. The walls were covered in beer signs and liquor posters. The carpet was red, but so worn and stained it looked more the color of dried blood. She tried to perk it up with a quick back-and-forth with the Bissel sweeper, but it made no impact.

Wobbly barstools were covered in red synthetic leather, their cracks mended with silver duct tape. A huge bar-length mirror behind the call drinks helped sooth any claustrophobia over the fact the bar was a galley only about twelve feet wide by forty feet long. Brandy quickly spritzed the mirror with Windex and wiped it clean with a dry coffee filter—one of her favorite insider tricks for streakless gleaming glass.

She then quickly raced around the high-top and low-top bar tables giving them a quick swipe with warm soapy water. She did the same to the full-size jukebox and two electronic dart game machines. Finally, she turned on the lone thirty-six inch flat-screen TV that was anchored a few inches from the ceiling off to the side of the bar mirror.

"What do you want to watch, Brownout?" she asked.

Brownout negotiated the channel selection with his fellow beer drinkers while Brandy counted the cash from last night's bank bag and placed it in the cash register drawer.

Big Joe, another "frequent flier" as Brandy liked to call her regulars, insisted on buying the first round for the high-nooners. Brownout protested, saying the first round was on him, but Big Joe got his credit card into Brandy's hands first while Brownout pretended convincingly to fumble with his wallet.

"Ah, you beat me again, Joe!" Brownout said, as he laughed and slapped his palm on the bar.

"Maybe next time, huh, Brownout?" Brandy said as she swiped Big Joe's credit card. The men continued to bicker over whose turn it would be to buy the next round while Brandy swiped and swiped again.

"Maybe your time is now, Brownout," she announced as she dropped Big Joe's card back on the bar. "The scanner won't take your card, Joe."

Brownout looked through his thin wallet. "G.D.!" he exclaimed, refusing to take the Lord's name in vain. "I can't find it. I must have left it at home!"

A chorus of "oh, yeah" and "sure you did!" erupted as Ralph stepped up to pay for the first round. Ralph was not his real name, of course, but a polite euphemism for regurgitation—which he was prone to do after too many of his favorite Chopin and seltzers.

Brandy returned to the card scanner next to the cash register on the back side of the bar. Brownout and the other high-nooners ribbed Big Joe mercilessly about his credit card being denied, speculating he'd blown through his credit limit on everything from fishing tackle to loose women.

"They take credit cards now?" Brandy said, eavesdropping on their conversation.

"Who?" Brownout asked.

"These loose women you all seem to know so much about."

"Oh, I wouldn't know about that," Brownout said, begging off. "But you can buy things nowadays and you don't even need a card. They just scan your phone, or you just type in somebody's phone number or email address and somehow your money just flies out of your bank account into their account. It's crazy. I learned it from my good-for-nothing daughter always asking me for money. That's why I don't carry cash. She used to always come and take it from me. I thought, 'if I don't have cash on me, there's nothing for her to sweet talk me out of' but now she taught me how I can just give it to her on my phone."

"Well, we might need to give that a try," Brandy said as she slapped down Ralph's credit card in front of him. "Ralph's card didn't work either."

There was a chorus of accusatory "Ohhhhs," and Big Joe got in a few shots.

"See, I'm not the only one!" he said.

They were incredulous that both their cards had been rejected. Brandy worried that her card reader might be broken. That would be just her luck.

"Let me try something," she said. She went to her purse and pulled out her trusty and well-worn VISA. She ran it through.

Denied.

"What?!" she shrieked. "Dammit! I think the card-reader's on the fritz. I'm going to have to call Richie Rich to get us a new one. He better get off his ascot and get back here before the bank closes. If I have to go all weekend without a card-reader I swear I'm . . ."

"You're what?" Brownout asked, calling her bluff.

"I'm gonna have to let you all drink for free!"

They erupted into applause and high-fives.

"Just kidding," she said as they all groaned good-naturedly.

CHAPTER THREE

With everyone's whistles wetted, Brandy finally relaxed behind the bar while Hairy made his rounds to the customers like a concerned Maitre'd ensuring everyone had a pleasant experience. His special brand of customer service included offering up a pat on his head or scratch under his chin. He was a sweet and goofy dog, but fiercely loyal to and protective of Brandy—and could go from zero to Cujo in an instant if the situation called for it. But he knew all the regulars and all the regulars knew him—in fact, he had his own loyal customers who came to the bar just for a dog-fix and to drink with the comfort of a furry friend to pet. He was a big draw at the bar . . . but also their best-kept secret.

The health inspector didn't know Hairy came to work with Brandy every day. If he did, "Olive or Twist" would be written up and fined at best and shut down at worst—and in either situation, Brandy would be forced to leave Hairy at home. She couldn't bear the thought of him being home alone and bored all day and she also felt vulnerable and insecure without him. He served as the de facto "bouncer" at the bar—he kept some of the more unseemly patrons in check due to his sheer size. On more than a couple of occasions, he had growled and barked unruly drunks out of the bar and onto the street. So, Brandy and her bar-goers had a tacit agreement: hide Hairy from the health inspector or be forced to slum it at "Liquid Larry's." Nobody wanted that.

Now that Brandy's Benny-Hill-madcap-chase of a morning had settled down, she decided to lean on her patrons for some unlicensed therapy.

"So, get a load of this," she exclaimed, as everyone sat down their drinks to listen. She proceeded to give a very animated blow-by-blow of the night before and how she and her friends had inadvertently stumbled upon Eric cheating red-handed when they were merely trying to ensure his safety.

"I see where this is going," Brownout interrupted. "I'm flattered. I know I'm easy on the eyes and now that you're single again it's understandable you'd put me at the front of the line. But I'm not ready for a commitment. I need to sew my wild oats."

The other regulars laughed, and Brandy nearly choked on the Diet Coke she was drinking.

"You think I'm telling you my sordid tale of woe as a come on?" She laughed until she had tears in her eyes. "What? Are you going to take me out on your 10-speed and show me around West Allis? Maybe we can go to the gas station on our first date to buy some scratch tickets."

Brownout sat with a satisfied grin, enjoying the rise he got out of everyone.

"And what are you talking about 'sewing your wild oats?' You're, like, sixty-five years old. You should have that out of your system by now."

"The ladies love my bike," Brownout said in his own defense.

"Well, I'm off bike enthusiasts. Eric customized motorcycles. Bike guys are nothing but trouble."

Her rapt audience was universally sympathetic.

"Who needs him?" "You're better off without him!" "He doesn't deserve you."

They also agreed Brandy was pretty enough and smart enough to have any guy she wanted, so while they empathized with her sadness and humiliation, they didn't feel sorry for her.

The heavy front bar door opened, sending a white-hot laser beam of sunlight into the darkened bar. Brandy could see only a silhouette of someone coming inside but could immediately tell, that someone was Chief Rivas.

The West Allis police chief had been like family to Brandy and her siblings throughout their lives and after their father and the Chief's best friend had died, he became a father figure, as well. He often stopped into the bar, almost daily, in fact, just to "check on things" and to have "just one or two" beers . . . or maybe five or six.

"Hey, Papí!" Brandy shouted, using a term of endearment from his Mexican culture. "So, I suppose you heard?"

"What? That you called a couple of my guys over to break-down Eric's door in the middle of the night? No, I didn't hear anything about that," he said with a wink.

"Well, I didn't mean to," she said sliding him a bottle of Modelo.

"He's lucky I didn't respond to the call. Officer Eisley said you gave Eric a hammer fist to the cajones. Let's just say, I would have done more than that."

Loretta and her husband, Smiley, approached the bar.

"You ready to close out your tab, Loretta?"

"Yes, ma'am. Did you get your machine working? I heard you saying something about your cash register being broken."

"Oh no, not the cash register. The credit card reader. The cash register's fine. I can take cash. I just can't take credit or debit right now. Richie Rich is supposed to go to the bank to swap it out."

Brandy had a thought. "Do you have a card I can try, Loretta? Maybe our internet is down. Those things run online, so when the internet is down, they don't work."

Loretta gave Brandy a credit card. After two seconds of anxiety, it was approved.

"Yay!" Brandy declared. "It's working again! We're back in business."

The bar erupted into applause.

As Loretta signed her receipt, Brandy explained to the Chief that her credit card reader had been acting temperamental. She thought it was broken, but apparently, it was working again. She shrugged it off, but the Chief was concerned.

"We've been getting calls about that. Has that been happening a lot?"

"What? Our credit card machine not working? Not that I know of. Today's the first time."

"Well, keep an eye on it. You might have been crowd hacked."

"What is that?"

"Electronic pickpocketed. Some punks build a card reader and it can scan credit cards. They'll walk past you in a crowd or walk up behind you at the grocery store. You won't even know it happened until your card doesn't work and all your credit's been used up. Some of the more powerful scanners can nab every card within forty-five feet. They can wipe out an entire restaurant or dentist office before anyone knows what happened."

"G.D.," Brownout said, "You can't carry cash, you can't carry credit cards. Nothing is safe. Maybe my daughter had the right idea—pay with your phone, then nobody can hack it. First good idea she had in ten years," then turning to the Chief as if to clarify he said, "my kid's an idiot."

"You might want to check your credit card balances," the Chief said. "Better to be safe than sorry. Because these guys are almost impossible to catch. By the time you realize you've been pickpocketed, you've been to the mall, you've been to the grocery store, you've been to Olive Garden."

"You mean 'Olive or Twist,' Papí," Brandy corrected.

"No, I meant Olive Garden. The restaurant—the one on Bluemound Road."

"Ohhh, ok. Gotcha."

"Anyway, you've been so many places we don't know where to start. People call to file a report, but we can't go round up everybody in every store or try to hunt down every car at every stoplight they sat next to. It's impossible."

"Nothing's impossible," Brandy said.

"Damn near impossible. I'd be a hero if I could catch even one electronic pickpocket. But they hide in plain sight and know there is safety in numbers. So, just watch yourselves. A bar like this would be a prime target."

"They wouldn't dare. Not with you around, Chief," Big Joe said confidently.

"Hey, aren't my taxes paying you to fight crime?" Brownout said. "We aren't paying you to drink in some dive bar all afternoon. Aren't you supposed to be investigating a crime somewhere?" Brownout could be prickly, still, it was hard to tell if he was joking or not.

"I am investigating a crime. Didn't you hear? The prettiest lady in town just got dumped," the Chief said raising his empty beer bottle in a phantom toast to Brandy.

"Alright, then you can stay," Brownout said.

*   *   *

It was nearing the end of her shift and Brandy was starving. She tacitly cursed Ginny for not helping her. *She's probably home braiding her hair and watching old reruns of the Carol Burnett show.* The bar didn't serve food—unless you count the pickled eggs in a small glass barrel, or the single-serving chips clipped to a rack behind the bar. She kept several cans of dog food in stock for Hairy and chided herself for never having the time or the energy to pack a lunch for herself. Her friend and co-worker, Matt, would be arriving soon for the changing of the guard. Brandy decided to order a pizza for them to share.

Matt arrived just a few minutes before 7:00 p.m. and was excited to hear dinner was on the way.

"Awesome! Thank you, Brandy! You must have read my mind. I was thinking of ordering food on my way over. I'm glad you did it."

"My pleasure," she said.

Matt was closer to Ginny's age than to Brandy's. They had worked together for several years. He was like the little brother she never had—and never wanted. She would tease Matt by telling him as much. Their titles were unofficial and self-assigned. Brandy acted as something of a general manager of the bar and Matt was her assistant manager. Chaz was the absentee owner and they weren't exactly complaining. They could schedule themselves as they pleased, and they covered for each other upon request.

There were two other weekend bartenders who rounded out the staff and helped fill in the gaps. First was Darbie, who was as young and cute as her name suggested. She was also a masterclass in laziness and manipulation. She refused to do anything for herself that someone else could do for her. But the bar patrons liked her because she was attractive and flirtatious. Her tips reflected her popularity.

The other part-time bartender was Virgie. She was a career bartender. She had seen it all and lived to tell about it. She was about a thousand years old but was spry as a mountain goat—and even looked a little like one. She had three white wiry hairs growing out of her chin to match the silvery updo that she got done at the "beauty parlor" once a week. Bar regulars called her "The Judge" because she had not a minute to spare for anyone's "bull malarkey" as she liked to call it.

While they waited for their pizza, Brandy filled Matt in on the events of the day—that Chaz had stopped by in the morning and that the credit card machine was acting up. She relayed what the Chief had said in warning about electronic pickpocketing, but still thought switching out the machine would solve the problem.

Soon a pizza delivery man swooped in the side door. "Hey! Look who's here!" Brandy announced.

Ordering end-of-shift pizza from "Pizza D'Action" was always a treat, mostly because their pizza was top-notch, but also because they had a revolving door of hot delivery guys. Brandy didn't recognize tonight's deliveryman—which meant he likely had never seen her hanging out at the bar with Eric after a shift when they would often order pizza together.

She tried to muster the poise to flirt—but she didn't know how. She hadn't flirted with anyone in two years. Her flirter was broke.

Matt almost ruined it for her when he tried to pay for the pizza.

"Don't worry doll face, tonight's on me," he said in an old-timey Humphry Bogart voice.

Worried the pizza guy would think they were a couple, she quickly chimed in.

"Oh no. Consider it a shift meal. As a 'thank you' to my best employee for an honest day's work."

She then handed Pizza Guy her credit card and heaved her breasts up onto the bar between clasped hands as she rested her elbows. Ginny's admonition haunted her. *You have more going for you than your breasts? You know that, right?* Brandy slunk from the bar and stood self-consciously with her arms crossed in front of her.

"Do you have another card? This one isn't working," Mr. Gorgeous said.

"Seriously? Ugh," Brandy said in frustration. "Does that thing run on wi-fi?" she asked, gesturing to a little handheld card reader in his hand. "Because my card reader didn't work earlier either. I think our wi-fi might be cutting in and out."

"I don't know," he said.

"Try it again," she suggested.

"It seems to be working," he said, "But it said the card is denied. It's giving me a denial code, but I don't know what it means."

"Here," Matt said, rescuing Brandy with some cash.

"Thanks," the guy said as he started making change for Matt.

"Oh no, that's for you. Just keep it."

"Thanks, man," he said giving them both a wave as he turned and left.

"This is bugging me," Brandy said. "Matt, try to go on your phone. Can you get on the internet?"

He could. And so could she.

"I have one more experiment. Ring up a fake transaction and then try to pay it with your card. We'll just cancel it, or I can just give you cash out of the drawer. Just ring up eight bucks."

Matt did as Brandy suggested. His credit card sailed through with no problem.

"Ok. Now do the same thing with mine," she said.

She stood nearly on top of him watching his every move to make sure he didn't do anything to inadvertently influence the transaction.

"Denied," he said.

She breathed a big sigh. She immediately started tapping away on her phone screen.

"What are you doing?" Matt asked.

"I'm checking my credit card balance. I'm beginning to think the Chief might be right."

Now Matt stood over Brandy, watching with anticipation. After flipping through a few screens, she nearly dropped the phone in anger.

"God dam . . ." she started before realizing Brownout was sitting right in front of her. "Sorry, Brownout."

"No worries," he said without even looking at her, eyes fixed on the television above her head.

"What?" Matt begged.

"My card! It's maxed out! Look at this!" She scrolled through a dozen transactions. "Those aren't mine! This is insane!"

She tapped out of the banking app and started punching in a phone number.

"Who are you calling?" Matt asked.

"I'm calling the Chief. I'm going to file a police report. This is outright theft. I can't believe this!"

"Maybe you should call the credit card company first and cancel your card," Matt advised, but she was already speaking to someone on the other end of the phone.

Matt didn't have any Twizzlers or popcorn to munch as he watched the drama unfold, so he dug into the pizza box.

"I just called the non-emergency number. They're sending somebody over," Brandy said.

"I thought you said the Chief told you they can't do anything. Just call the card company. Don't you have fraud protection? You aren't actually responsible for all those charges. Let the credit card company deal with it."

"Oh, Matt," she said in a patronizing voice that even Ginny would have envied. "You're adorable. They don't just steal your credit card number. They could have my pin number; they can steal my identity. And what really makes me mad is that the Chief acted like nobody could do anything about it. I think he's sending someone over here as a favor."

Brandy's phone started ringing. She looked down at it and then threw her head back in disgust.

"Ugh! It's him again." She turned her phone screen to face Matt where he could clearly see the caller I.D. said

"Eric." "He's been trying to call me all day. I'm not talking to him."

She looked down at the phone as it continued to ring.

"Here," she said, handing the phone to Ralph who could now barely focus his eyes, "it's your wife."

Ralph took the phone and awkwardly fumbled it, holding the screen facing out so he was listening to the phone case.

"What?" he yelled. "Speak up!"

Meanwhile, Brandy and Matt could hear Eric talking on the other end.

"Brandy, just listen to me. I just want to talk to you."

"I'll be home when I damn well feel like it," Ralph slurred. "Ok. In one hour," he said holding up one finger—that looked like two through his beer goggles.

"Brandy, Baby . . ." Eric continued to plead.

"I'm not talking to you!" she yelled in Ralph's direction.

"Calm down. Come here. Eat some pizza," Matt said.

"Oh, calm down? Why, I didn't even think of that!" she said sarcastically. "Pro-tip: In the history of the world, there is not one woman who 'calmed down' because a man told her to."

CHAPTER FOUR

Brandy was mad she had to stay at work and wait for the police officer to come take a report. She was still exhausted from the night before—something she explained to Matt sparing no detail. She'd had nothing to eat except for what was now some lukewarm pizza. Her hair was greasy. She needed a shower. And now all her credit had been siphoned away. What else could go wrong?

A cool breeze rushed through the front door with the answer. Coming toward her was James Fraley, Health Inspector.

"What's he doing here?" Brandy whispered to Matt as she sprung to action. "It's after 7 p.m. on a Friday night! I'll be at Carmen's. Text me when he's gone."

Brandy discreetly snapped her fingers and Hairy followed her from behind the bar through a back hallway into a stairwell that led to the apartment attached to the back of the bar. Hairy knew the drill. They'd been running it for ages.

They slipped out the back and went up the stairs to the interior apartment door and knocked.

Carmen answered in a bikini top and cut off jean shorts. She and her boyfriend, Doug, lived in the apartment. Brandy always marveled at what a mismatch they were. Carmen was young and beautiful like a Russian model while Doug was overweight, about twenty years older than her (by the looks of it), and, from all outward appearances, almost homicidally perturbed by everything Carmen did. But Carmen didn't seem to notice. If anything, it endeared him more.

"Hi Brandy, come on in. Is the inspector here again?"

"You got it."

"Baby!" she yelled to Doug from the doorway. "Brandy is here. Do you want to see Hairy?"

"Come here, Hairy!" Doug yelled from a recliner in the living room. "Hey, Brandy," he said, not bothering to get up.

Carmen carefully picked up the remote control and started clicking buttons with her long fingernails. "Do you want me to turn it down, so we can talk?" she asked Doug.

He sighed as if he had just explained something to a five-year-old a thousand times.

"I don't care," he said.

"Baby, be nice!" she said in a fake pouty voice. "Up or down?" she asked still holding the remote.

"Just give it here," he said, plainly annoyed. Brandy sat at their dining room table, uncomfortable with their exchange. But Carmen was oblivious. As she handed him the remote, she tried to tousle Doug's hair and he flinched away as if a bird had swooped at him. Meanwhile, he lovingly stroked Hairy's head.

"Do you guys need anything while I'm here?" Brandy asked "Is everything going ok? Did you see Chaz this morning?"

Chaz was their landlord. Technically, their landlord was Chaz's trust fund, but Brandy was its proxy given Chaz's general unavailability and disinterest. Brandy knew the value of having good tenants on site—they were a crime deterrent and another set of eyes in case the air conditioning unit crapped out and started leaking water. Doug and Carmen had only lived there for about three months, but they hadn't given Brandy any trouble.

"Yeah, Chaz stopped by to pick up the rent check. He seems to always find time for that," Carmen said as she rolled her eyes. "Otherwise, we're good. No complaints."

Brandy's phone buzzed. It was Matt telling her the coast was clear.

"Alright," Brandy said. "He's gone."

"Why did he come so late?" Even Carmen knew it was unusual for a health inspector to show up unannounced after 5 p.m. on a Friday night. "And why are you here so late? Were you supposed to meet with him or something?"

Brandy couldn't help but commiserate with Carmen about the unfortunate events of the preceding night—and how her credit card was stolen on top of it. She explained that she was now stuck at work waiting for a police officer to come take a statement so she could file a theft report.

Her phone buzzed again.

"Aaaand, that's him," she said as she checked her message. "Matt said the cop is waiting for me downstairs, so I better go. Thanks for letting us hide out for a few minutes."

"Sure, no problem," Carmen said.

"Bye, Hairy!" Doug yelled from his throne.

Brandy led Hairy back downstairs. Her legs hurt. It had been such a long day and an even longer night. She couldn't wait to go home. But as she rounded the corner from the hallway to the bar, she caught a glimpse of the police officer and decided she had nothing but time.

The cop was gorgeous. Even better looking than Pizza Guy. He almost didn't look like a real cop—he looked like a stripper cop or the model on the front of a romance novel about a cop. Brandy was awestruck.

She was also suddenly and painfully aware that she looked like someone dressed as a fart as for Halloween. Again, just her luck: Adonis arrives to take her statement when she looks her worst.

She decided to own it. But first, she needed a little liquid courage. She poured herself a shot of rum, tossed it back, shook her head, smoothed her ponytail, and approached Officer Charming at the end of the bar.

"Are you Ms. Alexander?" he asked. Brandy swooned. His teeth were so straight and white.

"Yes, thank you for coming over."

Brandy started at the beginning—when she swiped Big Joe's credit card and it was denied. She was painstaking with her details. The Chief always told her she would make a great witness. As she spoke, the officer took notes. He asked few questions which disheartened Brandy. She took it to mean he wasn't very interested and that he was just there to look like he was investigating. Or maybe he was only there because the Chief sent him. Either way, Brandy was going to make him work. She was going to make sure he took her seriously. She told him everything—pausing to ensure he kept writing.

As she talked, she noticed he kept glancing up at her. At first, she thought he was just being professional and making eye contact to show he was listening. But then she thought maybe he was being coy. She noticed he didn't wear a wedding ring. She hadn't had to read a man's signals for two years. She tried to rev-up her internal radar, even if she didn't entirely trust it.

At one point, she stopped mid-sentence and said, "What?" calling him out during one of his glance-ups.

"Oh. Nothing," he said, seeming embarrassed. "I was just getting distracted . . . " he trailed off as he gestured toward her face.

Oooh! Distracted? That didn't sound all bad. Maybe he thought she was pretty? Maybe he wanted to praise how well she was telling her story. She forged ahead with new confidence—even though she smelled like beer and a grease trap.

When he was done taking her statement, he gave her the same apologetic speech the Chief had given her about how difficult it was to catch electronic pickpockets or identity thieves and that, unfortunately, they were low priority crimes.

"So, I just sat here for an hour and a half past my shift, starving and half-asleep to tell you my story and you're telling me it doesn't matter, and you can't do anything about it?"

"No, that's not . . ." he stammered.

"I've lost almost $5,000 of credit, my identity is probably already for sale on the dark web, and you're merely flattering me by taking my statement?"

Brandy's voice was getting louder and people at the bar were starting to watch them.

"Ma'am," the officer said calmly. "All I meant to say is not to expect miracles. It's likely whoever did this will never be caught. It doesn't mean we won't try, but we have to prioritize violent cases and cases that can be solved. We can't spin our wheels on these things, so just don't expect a quick turn around on this."

"Well, then I'll find them myself. You can go deal with your violent crimes and I'll do your job for you."

"You really shouldn't try to hunt down criminals on your own. You don't know who you'll come across. I have to recommend you let us handle it."

"But you just said you're not going to handle it. Or, you're going to handle it on your own sweet time when you're done finding stolen bikes and rescuing kittens from trees. Well, that's not good enough for me."

"I'm sorry, Ma'am. It's the best I can do. I'm going to type this up. We'll have a detective call you from the fraud and financial crimes division. I'm just the note-taker tonight. If you want, you can pick up a copy of the report in the morning. Will you be able to do that?"

"The question is whether *you'll* be able to do that. You think you'll have time to prepare that report with all the 'real' crimes you have to solve?" Brandy was more than indignant.

The officer, again, studied her face then gave her a smile and bid her good night.

"Oh. I almost forgot," he said as he turned around and handed her his business card.

Brandy looked at his name.

"Is this for real?" she said, laughing.

"'Fraid so. I get it everywhere I go." The card said, "Officer Peter Dixon."

"I used to be a paralegal in my former life. There was this lawyer whose last name was 'Peckerman.' I always thought it was apt. Kind of like a chef with the last name, 'Cook,' or a financial advisor with the last name, 'Banks.' Maybe you and this Peckerman guy can start a support group."

He chuckled and gave her a subtle wave as he turned to leave.

He barely made it out the front door when Brandy grabbed her purse and called for Hairy.

"I'm outta here," she said to Matt.

He gave her a nod of acknowledgment from behind the bar as she marched out the side door. About three seconds later, she came back inside.

"What are you doing here?" Matt asked. "I thought you were done."

"I forgot, I don't have my car. My sister dropped me off. Now I have to wait for a stupid Uber."

If there was any Karma in the universe, Brandy was just about due for a streak of amazing good luck.

*   *   *

Brandy finally arrived home. It was a little after 9 p.m. Hairy had been walking around all day visiting with customers. Still, Brandy took him on a little spin around the block—more for herself than for him. She was still fired up over the notion someone could steal her credit—and possibly her identity—and it was all on *her* to do something about it. She's the one who would have to sit on hold with the credit card company and the fraud department. She's the one who would have to wait seven to fourteen business days for a new credit card to arrive. She's the one that would have to uncover any identity theft. She couldn't believe the cops' policy was to just throw-up their hands. She was concerned that Big Joe and some of her other bar patrons could be victims too. She wasn't going to stand for it.

After their walk, she got Hairy situated and went to the bathroom to take a shower. She caught a glimpse of herself in the mirror and shrieked in horror.

"Oh no! My tooth!" she squealed. "What happened to my tooth?"

She leaned into the mirror as if getting a closer look would reveal the gaping hole in the front of her smile was just a mirage.

Brandy had lost one of her top front teeth when she and Emily had dabbled in roller-derby in their twenties. It was a fun hobby at the time, but a couple years of it was enough. Brandy would always have a fake tooth as a memento of her time on the "Shevil Knevils."

She quickly called Matt.

"Hey, did you notice my tooth was missing at any point when you were talking to me?"

Brandy's tooth had traveled many journies around the bar. It had fallen into drinks. It had fallen into the ice bin. Matt had even had the privilege of babysitting it once when Brandy said, "hold my tooth," before diving into the fray to break up a bar fight. Little did the health inspector know, but Hairy was the least of his worries.

"No. I didn't notice," Matt said.

"Dammit," she sighed. "Well, don't take the trash out to the dumpster tonight. We're going to have to sort through it in the morning."

"I think you mean *you're* going to have to sort through it."

"Bye," she said sternly.

As soon as she hung up the phone, Brandy came to the awful realization that the gorgeous police officer kept looking up at her and was "distracted" . . . by her missing tooth. It was then, that she also realized there would be no Karma for her.

CHAPTER FIVE

Brandy called Emily first thing in the morning.

"Hey! I need you to come help me find my tooth."

"Where are you?" Emily asked. This was not her first tooth-finding mission.

"I'm on my way to the bar. I have to open. I lost it last night, so I need to find it before people start showing up.

"Alright, let me throw on some heels and I'll be right over."

Brandy was surprised Emily wasn't already wearing heels. She wore them all the time and claimed that, to her, they were more comfortable than sneakers or flip-flops or any kind of flat shoes. She wore them out at night, she wore them to the grocery store, she wore them to the dog park. She even had high-heeled snow boots. Brandy wouldn't have been surprised to learn Emily slept in them, too.

Emily actually beat Brandy to the bar. She was standing outside the side door with her back against the wall—her legs outstretched in front of her.

"Catching some rays?" Brandy asked as she got out of her car.

"Ugh. I'm so pale!" Emily said, even though her skin was the orangey-brown color of espresso with a splash of milk.

"You're going to get skin cancer," Brandy said.

"I don't go in tanning beds anymore. I use that foam stuff-it's like tanning lotion. It is ah-mazing! It doesn't look streaky or orangey or anything."

"Who told you that?" Brandy joked.

"Hardy har har," Emily said.

As Brandy rifled through a key-ring stuffed full of keys, Brownout came around the corner on his bicycle—the only form of transportation available to him after three OWI arrests. He was probably still technically "operating while intoxicated," but could do far less damage on a bike. And he refused to take the bus even though it stopped within stumbling distance of the bar's front door.

"You open yet, Miss Brandy?"

"Almost. You're early today, Brownout."

"It's 11:00 a.m. somewhere in the world! I'd say I'm right on time. Miller Time, that is," he said as he laughed at his own joke.

"How'dy do, Emily?" Brownout said.

"I'm good."

"You here to buy me a drink?" he asked.

"Not today. I'm helping Brandy find her tooth."

Brandy pushed open the door and led Emily and Brownout inside.

"I told Matt not to take the trash to the dumpster to make it easier to look through. He better not have forgotten."

"We're digging through the trash?" Emily asked.

"Um, *you're* digging through the trash. I have a checklist a mile long before I can officially 'open.' That's why I needed you to help. I can't look for my tooth and do all the opening chores at the same time. And once people start coming in, I'll be tied up. So, less talk, more rock. Get digging."

Emily stood frozen by two loosely tied garbage bags.

"Mmmph," she whimpered like a puppy.

Brandy went about her business pretending not to hear Emily's tepid protest.

Then Emily turned to Brownout.

"Garyyyy," she cooed. He loved that she used his real name. "Can you help me dig through this trash to find Brandy's tooth?"

Brownout felt like a knight in shining armor. He proudly stepped behind the bar.

"Step aside, little lady."

To say the two of them searched and sorted would be overselling it a bit. Mostly, Brownout searched while Emily "helped" by supervising and offering encouragement. Meanwhile, Brandy went about her list of opening tasks. Just as she was coming inside from watering her flowers, Brownout held his hand up in victory as if he had just extracted Excalibur from the stone.

"I found it!" he declared. Emily immediately reached up and attached her hand to Brownout's raised hand in order to share in the credit.

"We did it!" Emily squealed as she excitedly bounced up and down. She and Brownout hugged.

"I now pronounce you husband and wife," Brandy said.

"Ha! Ya hear that?" Brownout said to Emily. "How about a kiss for the groom?"

"Ew," she said. Brownout wasn't insulted. His pretend pursuit of Emily and her rejection of him was a running joke between them.

"You're welcome," Emily said as she did a little victory dance around Brandy.

"You didn't do anything except boss him around. Brownout," she said turning and bowing in reverence, "thank you. Your first drink is on me. Consider it your finder's fee."

"I'll take it!" he said excitedly.

Brandy checked the clock on the wall—an old Schlitz globe. Virgie would be arriving any minute. Brandy was a "key holder," meaning she had to open or close every day. Matt and Chaz had keys as well. So, she went in to open the bar, but she wasn't staying. It was Saturday, and she would have the day off for the most part. Virgie would work the early shift today.

Brandy plopped her fake tooth into a shot glass full of Listerine and poured Brownout a draft of Miller Lite.

"I don't know how you can drink that swill," she said as she made the Sign of the Cross and kissed the back of her thumb in order to stave off any curse she may have brought on herself by speaking ill of Our Lord and Savior Miller Lite. Miller Brewing Company had been a bedrock of Milwaukee's culture and economy for over one hundred years. It had a rabid and fiercely loyal local following. Some local bars refused to even carry the products of its main competitor, Budweiser. Brandy had nothing against Miller Lite, per se. It was beer in general that disagreed with her.

"You know I was going to marry you until you said that," Brownout said.

"Hey!" Emily barked. "I thought we were married."

"Ok. I'll be married to you then," Brownout said.

"I wasn't talking to you. I was talking to Brandy." They all laughed.

Virgie came in the side door as their chuckles were dying down. She was followed by her eleven-year-old great-grandson, Finn, who often came to work with Virgie when her babysitting shift overlapped with Finn's mom's work schedule. He'd sit at the bar and eat chips and play with Hairy until his Mom came to pick him up.

"Hey, Virgie," Brandy said. "Hi, Finn. How's it going?"

Finn hopped up on a stool at the end of the bar and sat on it with his knees curled under him so he could rest his elbows up on the bar and lean forward.

"Finn Patrick!" Virgie yelped. "Sit right on that stool! You're going to fall off and split your head open. Your mother and I don't have time for stitches."

He obediently wiggled his feet out from under him and sat side-saddle on the stool.

Virgie was fatalistic and operated under a world view based on extremes. She was sure she had one foot in the grave and the other one on a banana peel. She knew everyone else was dying too. That skin rash you have? Definitely lymphoma. That little cough just now? Your heart almost stopped, and that cough was your body reflexively restarting it. She got her hair done every week and every week she didn't die of a cerebral hemorrhage or stroke from resting the base of her skull on the hair-washing basin was another slim victory over certain death. Somehow, the irony of the fact she was approaching eighty years old and was still healthy and working was lost on her.

Today, she was complaining of a phantom itch on the inside of her upper right arm.

"Do you see that?" she said to Brandy. "Take a look there. What do you see?"

She exposed her arm just above the elbow and turned it outward for Brandy's unlicensed medical opinion. Brandy turned on the flashlight app on her phone in order to see it better in the bar's dim lighting.

"I hate to say it, but I think you're going to live to fight another day, Virgie. I don't see anything. No rash, no bumps, no bruise. Nothing."

"Exactly!" Virgie said. "That means it's probably a vertebra pressing on a nerve and it's causing an itchy sensation. It's a form of neuropathy. I think I have neurological damage."

"Let Hairy lick it!" Finn offered. "I read this story at school where a dog licked his owner and cured him because dog licks have healing properties."

"Well, what you should have read is the Milwaukee Journal. There was a man here in town, he got licked by his dog. Three hours later he was in septic shock because he got a bacterial infection from the dog saliva getting into a tiny little scratch he didn't even know he had. He had to get both his legs amputated and his hands—and part of his nose. So, don't let that dog lick you if you've been cut."

Brandy quietly considered whether Finn was going to grow up with anxiety over Virgie's constant insistence that death lurked around every corner. But he seemed to be a very smart and well-adjusted child.

Because of the powerful beer lobby in the state, children were allowed in local bars. Bars could choose on their own whether or not to impose age restrictions, but "Olive or Twist" didn't discriminate—especially when Finn was family and was only there for thirty minutes or so. Virgie liked to tease that she couldn't leave him home alone because he was so smart, he would build a bomb or hack the NSA if nobody was watching him. But, in fact, they lived quite a distance from the bar and once travel-time was included, both Virgie and Finn's mom felt it was too long for a fifth grader to be left alone. And Virgie likely harbored an irrational fear he would die of something catastrophic if he were unsupervised for an hour. Finn was only six years old when the arrangement started, but he liked coming to the bar. He liked helping run the cash register and he especially liked Hairy.

"Hey, Brandy," Finn said. "Do you have that list of expenses for office supplies? That's the only thing I'm missing to finish last month's books."

"Oh, shoot. I have the receipts, but I haven't gone through them."

"That's ok. I can go through them. It's fun," he said.

Finn was also the bar's unofficial bookkeeper. And he was a damn good one. He was a whiz at math and science and loved engineering and computers. He loved showing all the old men at the bar how to use their smartphones. He'd help them make the font bigger on the internet. He would help them download apps. But, his biggest contribution to their collective knowledge was in telling them about an online service that would allow them to make a phone call and send it directly to voicemail—never even chancing that the person on the other end would pick up. It was called "Slydial" and the men couldn't get enough of it. They could call their wives or bosses to tell them they would be home late or couldn't come to work the next morning with zero risk of an interrogation.

"Finn, I'm going to grab those receipts from the office. Otherwise, Virgie, are you good? Do you need me for anything else? Finn, can you keep an eye on Hairy for me? I have to go down to the police station and pick up my police report. I won't be long."

Brandy hadn't seen Virgie since the break-up and break-in involving Eric. Virgie also hadn't been warned about the suspected electronic pickpocketing. So, Brandy gave her the quick and dirty on all counts. Emily acted as an enthusiastic hype-man, shouting, "Yep! True story!" and "It was in-saaaane!" at high-points throughout Brandy's reenactment.

Virgie's reaction was predictable.

"He was probably going to murder you someday. You're better off. I've seen those *Dateline* shows and *Forensic Files*. It's always the boyfriend. I never liked him."

CHAPTER SIX

Emily accompanied Brandy to the police department on the off-chance Peter Dixon was working the front desk. Brandy thought he was cute and was desperate to redeem herself after looking like such a bum the night before but was afraid her "guydar" was off. She had been quietly berating herself for not figuring Eric out sooner and wondered how she could have been so blind. It had been a real blow to her self-esteem. She blamed him for being a total and complete loser, but she blamed herself for settling for such a loser. She didn't want to make the same mistake again. So, she needed Emily to come along—and to bring her objectivity.

On the way to the police department, Brandy was driving, and Emily was in the passenger seat. Brandy's phone rang and she asked Emily to check the caller I.D.

"It's him," Emily said. "He" needed no further explanation.

"He won't let up. He keeps trying to call me. I blocked his texts. But he keeps calling from other numbers too, so I just don't even answer my phone anymore."

"Oh!" Emily said suddenly. "That reminds me . . ." She pulled her purse from the floorboard and stuck her arm half-way in it, digging around.

"Ta-da!" she said, holding up a man's wallet. She opened it and started picking through it. She handed Brandy sixty dollars.

"This is your cut."

"Cut of what?" Brandy asked.

"While you were in Eric's bedroom playing Whack-a-Mole with his family jewels, I was raiding the living room. He cheated and I figure he has to pay. Literally. So, I stole his wallet."

"Oh my gosh, Emily! You are the best friend ever! I love it!" they laughed diabolically.

"Caroline can preach all she wants about tracking Danny on her friend-finder app, but that's child's play," Emily said. "She's an amateur. You can go through a man's phone, you can put a GPS on his car, but that won't tell you anything. A man's wallet tells ALL!"

Emily started digging through Eric's wallet. She pulled out cash and receipts. She looked over each one for clues—were any of them for restaurants? Fancy restaurants? Were there two entrees on the receipt? She dug some more. She flashed an unopened condom at Brandy and rolled her eyes.

"What is he? Fifteen? Jeez."

She also found scraps of paper haphazardly torn from a parent-piece of paper and scrawled with phone numbers and email addresses but with no names or businesses to indicate who the contact information belonged to.

"Very suspicious," Emily said.

She kept rooting through his wallet before suddenly and dramatically dropping both her hands into her lap like she had just found something shocking.

"What?" Brandy said. Emily stared straight ahead smiling. "What?" Brandy urged.

"This moron has a list of all his online passwords written on a little sheet of paper. Look! Facebook, Twitter, Tinder—Ew! Sorry, you had to hear that—Netflix, First National Bank . . ."

"Are you serious?" Brandy said, snapping the paper out of Emily's hand.

They were sitting at a stoplight as she glanced over it.

"Oh my gosh! What an idiot," Brandy said.

"I'll take that," Emily said slyly as she pinched the paper from Brandy's grip.

Emily was transferring all of this solid gold documentation—the scraps of paper, the list of passwords, even the condom—to her own purse. She then moved on to his credit cards.

"He's got four hundred dollars in pre-paid VISA cards in here. What's his deal? Doesn't he have his own credit card?"

"Yes. Far as I know, he does. I've seen him use it a million times. I guess I never looked that close, but it just looked like a normal credit card."

"Well, so do these. Does he have ten nieces graduating from high school? That's the only reason anyone should be carrying around four hundred dollars in VISA cards—is if you were going to put them in the mail as a gift."

"Do whores take VISA?" Brandy asked as Emily chuckled and gave her a high-five.

Then, Emily suddenly became serious.

"It's him, Brandy. He did it."

"What do you mean? Did what?"

"Look at this," she held up a credit card. "Look. Right here. Look whose name is on this card." Emily shoved it into Brandy's face.

"I'm driving, Emily, I can't read it," Brandy said, growing concerned.

"It says, Brandy Alexander. He's the one who stole your credit card! I have it right here in my hot little hand. We've caught him. He's busted!"

Brandy was furious. "I can't believe he would stoop so low. Or maybe I can. I don't even know anymore. But proof is proof. Let's go turn his butt in! I don't even need the police report now. We can just go in there and show them the card—that's in *my* name, in *his* wallet. Gah, I can't believe he's such a scumbag!"

"Are you crazy? We can't do that! They'll arrest *me*. I stole his wallet knowingly and intentionally. If we bust Eric for stealing your credit card, there's no way he's not going to press charges against me for stealing his wallet."

"So, what do we do?" Brandy said. The last thing she wanted to do was give Eric the satisfaction of getting Emily in trouble.

"Let me handle this. Give me your phone."

Brandy handed it over unquestioningly.

Emily scrolled through the phone app and dialed Eric's number. He immediately picked up the phone.

"Baby? Baby, listen to me . . ."

"I ain't your baby," Emily said sternly. "And your baby's all grown up now and isn't taking anymore of your crap. I hate that I have to even talk to your ugly lying face, but when we were grabbing up Brandy's stuff the other night—you know, the night you were passed out naked with a college girl? You remember that, right? Ok, good. Because I'm not going to let you forget it. Well, while you were tangled up with your Thursday night skank, I accidentally grabbed your wallet. So, if you want it back, you're going to have to come get it."

Brandy listened to Emily's end of the conversation whereby Emily negotiated to meet in the parking lot of Home Depot. Brandy knew immediately this was because Home Depot was convenient for Emily—it was close to the hair salon where she was a stylist—and inconvenient for Eric. Emily asked him whether he'd be in his car or on one of his motorcycles, so she'd know how to recognize him. She then confirmed it all.

"Okay. I'll see you today at 3 p.m. And don't be late because I have a client coming at 3:30 pm, so I don't have a very big window. Got it?"

Emily hung up the call and looked at Brandy with an evil grin.

"Mwah ha ha," she said in a low vampire voice.

"Are you actually going to give it back to him?" Brandy asked.

"Hell no. Like I said, he's going to pay. Starting with this," Emily said holding up a business card. "Looks like he was only one punch away from a free sub sandwich at City Subs. Looks like lunch is on Eric today!"

Brandy knew it was the ultimate insult. Eric coveted those punch cards and was very scrutinous about cashing them in.

"Emily, I love you," Brandy said blowing her an air kiss.

"I love you too, Schmoopy."

*   *   *

They arrived at the police department and approached the desk officer. Brandy thought they would have the report ready for her at the pick-up window, but the officer told her to take a seat in the waiting area.

She had tried to look presentable. She again had her hair in a high ponytail and wore natural makeup and a figure-hugging sundress. She had all her teeth today. Emily was striking and considered beautiful by all accounts, but Brandy could go toe-to-toe with her in the looks department any day of the week. Emily had medium-length auburn feathered hair that somehow managed to look chic and stylish even though the style hadn't changed since high school. She was tall and thin with a wide cleavage gap that hinted at the breast augmentation she'd had about ten years ago. Brandy was a natural beauty. Both of them looked damn good for being forty years old and still had to show their I.D.s on occasion. They "matched" as best friends and were a formidable pair.

When Brandy didn't see Officer Dixon at the front desk, she assumed she'd gotten all dolled up for nothing. But when she looked up from her phone, her heart started to race.

"Here he comes, here he comes," she whispered sideways to Emily.

"Hello! Brandy, right?" Officer Dixon said as he shook Brandy's hand. His grip was firm and professional. She looked him right in his dark brown eyes and smiled broadly—hoping to show him she didn't always have a hillbilly smile.

"Yes. Hi. And this is my best friend, Emily West."

Emily and Officer Dixon shook hands.

"Let's go over here and step out of the lobby," he said as he turned to show them to a pool of cubicles. When his back was to them, Emily gave Brandy a silent nod of approval. Brandy smiled and opened her mouth in a silent happy scream in return.

"Actually, could you point me in the direction of the restroom," Emily asked in a deliberate effort to leave Brandy and Officer Dixon alone.

"Oh sure. Go down that long hallway, turn right. The women's is the first door."

"Alright. Brandy, I'll just meet you back out here."

"Ok," Brandy said.

Officer Dixon showed Brandy to a desk. He sat down on one side and offered her an empty seat opposite him.

"So, how's your investigation going?" he asked her.

"I'm sorry. What investigation?" Brandy said.

"Last night, you swore you were going to launch your own investigation. I was just wondering how it's going," he said with a smirk.

Ohhh. He's teasing me. Brandy thought. But she wasn't sure if he was teasing her in the way a ten-year-old boy teases his crush or if was teasing her because he was being a jerk. So, she decided to show off a little bit. If he was being a jerk, she'd shut him down. If he was being coy, he would be impressed.

"As a matter of fact, I think I solved the case," she bragged.

"Oh really?" he said as if he were both intrigued and impressed.

"Yes. My ex-boyfriend. I think he either stole my credit card or took out a credit card in my name." Emily would kill her for outing her, and she was wary of Emily's reasonable fear about getting in trouble for stealing Eric's wallet, so she decided to invoke the same story Emily gave Eric if need be—that it was strictly accidental, and she was going to give it back.

"Is this the same ex-boyfriend you punched in the nuts after you called the fire department to break down his door?"

"Could be," Brandy said laughing at herself. "Then again, you might have me confused with someone else. That probably happens every night of the week."

She wondered how he knew about the situation and feared she was now the laughing stock of the whole police department.

"Good news travels fast," she said with an eye roll. "Were the police officers who responded talking about it? I'm so embarrassed."

"Oh no," he said. "I, uh, I asked about you." He nervously tapped a pen on the desk as he looked away.

"Who did you ask?" Brandy said, unable to suppress a smile.

"The Chief. I know he frequents your bar. That's probably a charitable way of saying it."

"Yeah, he's there quite a bit," Brandy conceded.

"Worst kept secret in town that the Chief spends half his time day-drinking at 'Olive or Twist.' But, um, yeah. I asked him about you."

"What did you ask?" she said, dying for more.

"I don't know," he said blushing. He was now trapped. He couldn't just abandon the discussion. "I just asked him what your situation was. He told me as of Thursday night you are single. I'm sorry if that seems forward. And I'm sorry to hear about your boyfriend. I'm sure it's been really hard. The Chief said you are like a daughter to him. That he's known your family forever." He was trying to move the subject away from his big "ask" to more neutral ground.

"Well, wow," Brandy said. "I'm flattered. I don't know what to say."

"Do you want me to go shake-down your ex? If he really did steal your credit card, I should probably go have a talk with him."

"I don't know if he did for sure. I mean, I'm pretty sure, but I don't want to accuse him if he didn't. And I never want to see him again. If I have to testify or see him in court or anything, I'll pass."

"I don't mind following up. It's my job. Besides, I kind of want to check out my competition," he said with a wink.

Brandy was reeling inside.

"Oh, he's no competition. Trust me. It's over for good."

He convinced Brandy to give him Eric's phone number and address and he elicited the fact Brandy had actually seen her credit card in his wallet. She didn't say that Emily had the wallet or anything that would incriminate her. She was careful to be economical with the truth.

After their conversation was over, he printed the police report she had come to pick up. He wrote something on it and slid it across the desk to her.

"I just put my number on there. In case you want to discuss the case over dinner sometime."

Brandy picked up the report and looked at the phone number written in blue ink. It took a second to register.

"My personal number," he said.

"Oh," Brandy said. Then with realization kicking in, she said, "Ohhh," and smiled broadly.

"You know. No pressure," he said.

"Thank you," she said, awkwardly rising from her chair.

"Ok, then," he said, suddenly switching into business mode. "If you have any questions about the report, just let me know. And if I find anything out from this Eric guy, I'll be sure to keep you posted."

Brandy was nearly speechless with delight. Did he just ask her out? Where was Emily? She was dying to spill her guts. Emily would know just what to do.

They emerged into the lobby. Emily was sitting on a bright yellow plastic chair scrolling through her phone. She looked up and could immediately tell from Brandy's expression that something big had just happened.

Brandy literally skipped to the car as Emily chased after her in her four-inch heels.

"What did he say?" she demanded.

Brandy manically regurgitated the entire conversation and waved the police report in Emily's face as they sat and commiserated in Brandy's car.

"Well, are you going to call him?"

"I don't know. I want to. But I don't know what to say."

"He put the ball in your court. He probably doesn't want to seem insensitive since you just got dumped. So, if you're not ready to jump back into a relationship, he'll let you bow out gracefully. He kind of saves face and lets you control the decision. It's a good move on his part. It shows some emotional intelligence. You haven't seen that in a while. I think you should call him. What have you got to lose?"

"I think I should ask Papí, first. Peter asked him about me. Maybe I should ask him about Peter."

"I like that you've already moved him to first-name-basis. That's trending in the right direction."

"I mean, on the other hand, he could be a serial killer."

"WWVD?" Emily said as she laughed. "What Would Virgie Do?"

"I'm kidding of course. But if his situation is complicated—ex-wife, four kids, lives with his mother . . ."

"Stop overthinking it."

"I'm not overthinking. I'm strategizing."

"Well, I'm not strategizing anything. I'm full-on scheming. And Eric and your little cop friend better not ruin it for me."

"I didn't tell him you have the wallet. I didn't say anything that could get you in trouble."

"Well, Eric knows I have it. So, if Officer Dreamy talks to him, he better not falsely claim I stole it."

"But you did steal it," Brandy said.

"Yeah, but he doesn't know that. He thinks it was an accident in the heat of the moment. Let him prove otherwise. Meanwhile, I'm sticking to my story. Anyway, I think Officer Dreamy is going to be on my side now. He's got a lady to impress."

"We'll see," Brandy said.

"The hell we will. We already saw. It's on!"

CHAPTER SEVEN

They drove back to "Olive or Twist" so Brandy could pick-up Hairy and drop Emily off at her car. She was excited to see the Chief was sitting with Brownout—but not surprised. It was nearly noon, after all.

Finn had already been picked up, but she didn't see Hairy anywhere.

"Hey, where's Hair—"

"Ix-nay on the Airy-hay," Virgie said. "Fraley's here."

"Ohhh," Brandy groaned. "What does he want?"

Health inspector, James Fraley was at the far end of the bar talking to a couple of the customers. Fortunately, everyone at the bar knew the drill, so Hairy was safely upstairs with Carmen and Doug.

"Hi, James," Brandy said trying to sound polite. "What brings you in on a Saturday?"

"I forgot my tablet. I thought maybe I left it here when I stopped by last night."

"I'm sorry I missed you. Was there anything in particular that you needed?" Brandy thought it was odd he had come by after hours last night and was hoping to elicit his motives without sounding defensive.

"Nah, I just realized that when I had come by earlier last week, I forgot to take the temperature readings from your beer cooler, and our software won't let me submit my report unless all the fields are filled out, so I had to come back by to take a reading. So, I know I had my tablet here with me last night, but now this morning I can't find it."

"I haven't seen it. If I do or if anyone finds it, I'll let you know."

As if he were skeptical, James decided he would have to look for himself. He walked around the back side of the bar and looked around and under the counters. He even looked inside the beer cooler. He then went to the back and poked his head in the back office. After he had scoured the place, he seemed satisfied.

"Welp. Let me know if you see it."

"Will do," Brandy said.

James left and Virgie went to retrieve Hairy. Meanwhile, Brandy made a beeline for the Chief.

"I just got back from picking up my police report. Guess who I saw?"

"Your future?" he asked with a laugh.

"I need all the dirt. I need to know everything. He gave me his number. I'm dying to call, but I don't want any drama. So, lay it on me."

"He came by my office first thing this morning and asked about you."

"I know. But what did he *sayyy*?" Brandy was going to settle for nothing less than a verbatim transcript.

"He said, 'Hey Chief, you know that bar on Adler— Olive or Twist? I said, 'I've been there a couple times.' He said, 'I took a statement from the bartender there. What's her story? Is she married?' I said, 'Oh no. There's no man good enough for her.' And then I told him what a good-for-nothing Eric was and how you dumped him in grand fashion and that you were the best catch in town, but he'd have to come through me first."

"Aww," Brandy swooned. "That's sweet of you."

"I also told him you got a sister who's better looking."

"You did not!" Brandy screeched as she reached over the bar to give him a playful slap on the shoulder. "So, what his deal? Does he have a dozen ex-wives? Ten kids? How is he single?"

"I don't know. He's a nice guy. Real smart. He's never given me any problems. I give you my blessing," he said as he waved his low-ball glass at her in the sign of the cross.

"If it don't work out, you always got me, Honey," Brownout said.

"I'll keep that in mind," Brandy said, even though they both knew she didn't mean it. "Come on, Hairy." He did an about-face and pranced the length of the bar to where Brandy was standing by the door.

"Oh, Virgie—before I go, is the credit card machine working today? Have you had any problems running cards?"

"Only Brownout's," Virgie said. "Because it's invisible."

Everyone roared as Brandy groaned at the joke and ushered Hairy out the door.

Once home, she called Ginny and invited her over for a late lunch or, in Ginny's case, an early dinner. Despite their age difference, Ginny had become a trusted confidante and the sisters had grown close as adults. Brandy spent most of her teenage years either babysitting Ginny or shooing her out of her bedroom. So, it was nice that they could finally have a "real" sister relationship.

Brandy whipped up some turkey, bacon, and avocado wraps that they could eat on the back patio while Hairy romped in the fenced-in back yard.

Ginny was enticed to come over by the promise of a big reveal about Brandy's love life.

"You better not have gotten back together with him," was Ginny's response.

After Brandy reassured her that would never happen and that her news was good news, Ginny agreed to come over. But Ginny knew what was coming. So, she thought she should at least try to be the voice of reason.

"It's a little soon to be jumping into a relationship, don't you think?" Ginny asked as they sat in the shade of the patio umbrella.

"I don't know. Is there a period of mourning I'm supposed to observe? Am I supposed to wear a black armband or something for a while?"

"You don't *need* a man," Ginny said. "Maybe just be single for a while. You might like it."

"Do you like it?" Brandy said, though she already knew the answer.

"We're not talking about me," Ginny said defensively.

Ginny had never had a boyfriend and wanted one desperately but was too socially awkward and too morally conservative to show her interest. Brandy half-suspected that Ginny wanted her to be single too in order to help justify her own single status. There was safety in numbers. It would be far more understandable for Ginny to be single if her older equally beautiful sister were single too.

And Brandy knew she didn't "need" a man. She just liked the dynamic of being coupled. Emily was her best friend and fulfilled most of her emotional needs—but not all of them. And she fulfilled none of her physical needs. Brandy just felt more personally well-rounded when she had a significant other.

It also provided a bit of insulation from creepers at the bar who might otherwise try to hit on her or get too cozy. Having a boyfriend made her off-limits for all but the most bold and obnoxious of customers—and Hairy knew how to handle them.

"So, you don't think I should call him?" Brandy asked.

"I think you should take some time for yourself. Were you wearing that dress when he gave you his number?"

"Yes."

"Then I'm not surprised."

"What's that supposed to mean?"

"It's a little short. He probably has, you know—*expectations*."

"Oh. You think I look like a slut? Well, I think you look like an off-duty nun."

"There's no such thing. Nuns are never off-duty."

"You better hope not. You better hope they're praying around the clock for you. That's the only way your

Prince Charming's ever going to show up. You need to make it happen. At least I'm putting myself out there."

Ginny rolled her eyes in the way that only little sisters can.

"Have you thought of staring pensively into a well?" Brandy said. "I hear that will make Prince Charming appear in a fortnight."

"Let it out. That's right. Let it all out. I'm here for you," Ginny said being exceedingly patronizing.

Hairy had come out of the grass to loiter between them as if he were trying to diffuse their dustup with his loveable presence.

"Well, if you are dead set on calling this guy back, I'm going to check him out," Ginny said. "I'm just putting that right up front. You don't have the best track record of exercising good judgment in the selection of partners, so I'm taking matters into my own hands."

"Papí already told me about him."

"Was he drunk when he said it?"

"Maybe," Brandy said, though the way she said it meant, "Yes. Totally. For sure."

"Then I'm going to do my own vetting."

Ginny fancied herself an amateur sleuth. She loved to read cozy mysteries—especially the ones about baking and witches. And because of them, she believed she could crack any case large or small.

"But just so you know," Brandy said, "even if you find out he comes from a long line of vampires destined to take over a small bed and breakfast on the shores of Lake Michigan—it's not a deal breaker for me."

CHAPTER EIGHT

Emily was in her dining room painting her toenails when the alarm on her phone startled her. It was almost 3:00 p.m. She turned off the alarm and without putting her phone down, she called 911.

"Hello? Yes, I'm driving south on Highway 100, I just passed the intersection of Greenfield Avenue. I'm behind a dark blue pick-up truck that is driving erratically. He's weaving in and out of lanes. He's cutting people off. Oh! Oh," she shrieked for dramatic effect. "He almost went up the curb. I think he may be drunk. Should I stay with him? Or what should I do?"

The dispatcher advised her to drop back, to not follow or confront the driver and the police were on their way.

"Ok, we're at a stoplight right by Home Depot."

The dispatcher thanked her, and Emily hung up the phone with a satisfied grin and waited.

As Eric neared Home Depot, two patrol cars raced up behind him. They tailgated him for a couple blocks and as he turned into the Home Depot parking lot, their flashing lights came on.

One officer approached Eric's driver side window.

"Sir, I need to see your license and registration."

Meanwhile, a second officer was on the passenger side of Eric's truck, heavily scanning the interior of his vehicle.

"What's going on?" Eric said.

"License and registration, sir."

"I don't have my license. That's why I'm here. I'm picking it up from somebody."

"So, you don't have a license on you? Or any kind of I.D.?"

"No. I lost my wallet. Well, I didn't actually lose it. Someone took it—some girl was at my house and grabbed it on accident. I'm supposed to meet her here to pick it up. She's probably here right now. She can tell you."

The cop at the passenger side continued to scrutinize the front and back of Eric's cab and did a walk around his truck bed as Eric watched nervously through the rearview mirror.

"May I ask what he's doing?"

"No. You may not. Worry about me, not him. You got it?"

"Yes sir," Eric said.

"Have you had anything to drink today sir?"

"What?" Eric said defensively. "No! This is ridiculous!"

"Oh, do you think so? Then you won't mind doing some ridiculous little tests. Sir, I'm going to need you to get out of the car. Keep your hands where I can see them."

"Why? What did I do? I don't get it?"

"We received a call from another motorist that you were driving erratically and endangering other drivers."

Eric angrily gripped the steering wheel. "Well, that's crap. I just got here. I swear, just let me find my friend—she's here. She has my I.D. then I can show it to you."

"Sir, keep your voice down and step out of the truck."

Eric muttered some expletives as he got out.

The officer had Eric perform a walk and turn up and down a painted parking lot line. A small crowd of onlookers had gathered to watch and film with their phones. Eric then had to stand on one foot and count out loud. Lastly, his eyes were closely scrutinized while following the movement of an ink pen.

One officer stood watch over Eric while the other one went back to his car to enter Eric's name into his computer.

"Can I at least call my friend? She's here somewhere waiting for me. Then she can at least bring me my wallet."

"No. You don't need to call anybody. You just stay put."

Eric stood there staring down his handler and occasionally protesting his detainment with colorful language.

After a couple of minutes, the police officer came back from his car and handed Eric a ticket.

"You're receiving a ticket today for operating without a license."

"But I have a license!" Eric yelled. "I just don't have it on me. It's probably in this parking lot as we speak. You just won't let me go get it."

"I can see in my computer that you have a valid license. But you have to carry it with you when you operate a motor vehicle. If you don't have it with you when I ask to see it, it's a two hundred and fifty dollar fine."

"Two hundred and fifty dollars!" Eric yelped. "Why can't you just give me a warning or make the ticket conditional on my showing you the license tomorrow? Hell, I can even bring it later today. I have a license!" he said drawing out the words as if he were trying to translate for someone who barely understood English.

"Sir, return to your vehicle and I suggest you take a deep breath before you drive anywhere. If we get another call about you tailgating or because you have some road-rage after this, that ticket is going to be the least of your problems."

Eric huffed as he climbed back in his truck. He immediately called Emily.

"Where are you?" he said angrily.

"Where are *you*?" she said from the comfort of her dining room table.

"I'm at Home Depot. I just got pulled over for some crap. I need my wallet."

"Well, I waited for you. It's 3:20 p.m. I told you I have a client at 3:30 p.m."

"I'm not driving all the way to your stupid salon."

"Hey," she said abruptly. "I don't care if you get your wallet back or not."

"I'm supposed to be on my way to a Brewer's game right now. I need my wallet!"

"Then come and get it," she said knowing full-well he wouldn't.

"Arrrgh," he yelled into the phone. "I'm picking it up TO-NIGHT. After the game." He was trying to assert himself, but he knew he had no power in this situation—or at least none he was willing to inconvenience himself to invoke. Emily knew he would rather go to the Brewers game and mooch off his friends—or his skank du jour—than hassle with driving all the way to a beauty salon.

"Ok, she said. Fine by me. Meet me at The Cage at 9:00 p.m."

"Where's that? What is The Cage?"

"It's a bar on National Avenue, just south of the stadium. See? I'm being nice to you by making it easy for you. So, you better be there this time. And on time! I'm not running all over town just to get your stupid wallet back to you."

"Fine. I'll be there at 9:00 p.m."

"Hey, quick question," Emily said. "Why do you have a credit card with Brandy's name on it in your wallet?"

"Have you been looking through it?" his voice was agitated and serious. "Don't go digging through there. That's none of your business. That's *my* stuff."

"All except for the free sub. That's mine now."

He hung up on her.

Emily laughed out loud at the plans she had in store for poor Eric.

*   *   *

Despite Ginny's warnings, Brandy made the call. Peter was clearly excited to hear from her but tried to play it cool. He

70

invited her to go to dinner at a "fancy" hipster bar called Lucky Joe's. He promised her an update on Eric.

"If that's okay," he quickly said. "That's not why I want to take you dinner. It's not a business meeting. And I don't want to open any old wounds. I just thought I'd fill you in and then we can shelve all that."

"No, no. That's totally fine," Brandy said.

So, later that night, they met up at Lucky Joe's.

When Brandy arrived at the bar, Peter was already there. She was happy to see that he was a little early. She took that as a sign of both eagerness and respect. This was starting off on the right foot. He stood up when she approached the antique wooden booth he had been seated at and seemed unsure if he should shake her hand or give her a hug in greeting, so he leaned in awkwardly for a little of both.

Brandy slid into the booth across from him and they enjoyed some small talk as she looked over the cocktail menu.

"I love craft cocktails," she said. "I don't really get to make them much at my bar. Everyone there is pretty set in their ways. I pour a lot of beer and wine. And Tito's Vodka. Nothing fancy likes these drinks."

Peter asked her for a recommendation and admitted he had no idea what half the ingredients in the cocktails even were. Cucumber tincture? Fat-washed Mezcal? He was a Miller Lite guy but wanted to impress her.

She quizzed him about different flavors and finally recommended a gin fizz for him. She ordered a "spirit forward" drink called a "Millionaire" for herself.

"Ok," Peter said as they waited for their drinks. "First things, first. Let's get Eric out of the way. Long story short, he says he didn't steal your credit card."

Brandy looked surprised and then settled in. "I think I want to hear the long version of this short story."

"After you came to the station, I called him. I asked if I could interview him because we had reason to believe he had been using credit in someone else's name without their consent. He acted all shocked and asked whose credit. I said, 'Brandy Alexander.' He said, 'Ahhh. I see where this is going.' He claimed you were just trying to get even with him. Then he seemed very interested in talking to me because he wanted to clear his name.

"So, I actually met up with him at his chop shop or whatever you call it. I told him that you had actually seen a credit card with your name on it in his wallet. He claimed it was totally innocent. He remembered you guys had gone out to eat and kind of fought over whose turn it was to pay and so you put your card in the sleeve or holder for the waitress but then went to the bathroom. So, he took your card out and put his card in so he could pay, but then forgot to give you your card back.

"That could be true," Brandy said. It sounded vaguely familiar.

"He swore he didn't use it. He asked what kind of transactions were on the card, implying they wouldn't match up with his normal spending habits. I didn't know the answer to that. But, as much as I hate to give the guy any credit, he seemed sincere."

"I could look at the transactions. There are a lot of them. I haven't really scrutinized them yet. I'm kind of afraid to look, to be honest."

"Ha," Peter chuckled. "But then get this—he tried to get me to help him. He said your friend Emily has his wallet and won't give it back. He asked if I could file a police report for theft."

"Oh, she didn't steal it," Brandy quickly offered up. "That night when we found him with his jail-bait we started gathering my stuff. Emily said she accidentally grabbed it. I'm sure she'll get it back to him."

"Then, nothing to see here, folks," Peter declared, satisfied with her explanation.

Their cocktails arrived and Peter complimented Brandy for the recommendation. He liked the gin fizz. After a couple drinks, he said, "So, I heard you asked the Chief about me." He cocked his head and gave her a coy smile.

"He told you?" Brandy said, acting shocked.

"Oh yeah. He told me you asked about me. And when I told him later that we were going to go out tonight, he gave me a big talking-to, just like a Dad about how I better treat you like gold."

"Awww, Papí," Brandy said. "I love him. He's been like a Dad to us."

"So, how often does he come into the bar? This is totally off the record. I'm not trying to get him in trouble or anything. But people talk around the department like he's a total alcoholic. He's always been very professional with me. I've never seen him drunk that I know of. So, I'm not sure what to believe. I thought I'd ask the opinion of an impartial third party."

"Well, I don't know how impartial I am. I would never say or do anything to undermine him. Is it bad? Like, do people not respect him because of it?"

"I'm not really on the inside of office politics. But I hear things. Little rumblings. From what I gather, they are trying to push him to retire so they don't have to fire him— but he refuses to quit. If they fire him, he'll lose his pension. But the bigger hit would be to his reputation. Don't tell him any of this. I can't believe I'm telling you all this. Again, we never had this conversation."

"Oh no. I won't say anything. I appreciate the information, though. You know what they say, 'knowledge is power.' Maybe I can gently steer him toward drinking less or spending less time in the bar? Yikes. I honestly don't know if that's possible."

"I wasn't meaning for you to do anything about it. Really. I was just making conversation. So, now you know my office gossip. Tell me some of yours. What goes on at 'Olive or Twist?'"

They had a nice conversation about all the regulars at the bar. Peter loved hearing about their unique quirks and personalities. He especially loved hearing about Hairy and asked if he could meet him sometime.

"So, does that mean you want to see me again?" Brandy asked.

"Of course," he said eagerly before reigning himself in. "That is if you want to see me again."

"Hmm. I don't know," she whined. His expression immediately fell as he tried to look unaffected. "I mean, you're a nice guy and all. It's just a pity you were born so handsome."

She couldn't keep the ruse going and laughed at herself. He laughed in relief.

"Did I have you going for a second?" Brandy asked as she batted her eyes.

"Hey, it takes a lot of luck for a guy with a mug like this to get a girl like you."

"Well rest assured, I would love to see you again."

The waitress delivered the check and after some obligatory, but pretend, negotiations over who would pay, Peter "won."

They continued to talk about their interests. Brandy told him about her friendship with Emily. Then the waitress returned.

"Sir, I'm sorry, but do you have a different card we can try? This one was denied."

Brandy felt embarrassed by association. She felt so bad for Peter. What a thing to have happen on a first date. She immediately came to his rescue.

"It's ok. We can use my card."

"Oh no," he said. "I'll just pay cash. It's not a big deal."

He gave the waitress a handful of money and she left the table.

"I don't get it though. That card has plenty of credit on it. It should work. And it's all paid up. I don't want you to think I don't pay my bills."

"Never," Brandy said. "I don't want to sound like a conspiracy theorist, but the Chief said you guys have been getting a lot of calls about stolen credit. Me included. Do you think someone could have hacked your card?"

"I guess anything's possible. But, some of these home-made card skimmers can steal every card within forty-five feet. So, for it to have happened to both of us, means it had to happen someplace we were in close proximity. Which would mean it either happened at the police department or at your bar."

"You're giving my customers way too much credit. I don't think any one of them has the technological prowess to build a credit card skimmer. They rely on an eleven-year-old to show them how to change the volume on their ringers."

"Then maybe you need to look at that eleven-year-old."

She laughed as if the idea were ridiculous.

"You'd be amazed what kids know these days," he said.

"Finn's too smart. He could probably build a rocket ship from table scraps, but he's not stupid enough to do something criminal. He's a good kid."

"Maybe he's just smart enough to not get caught."

"No," Brandy was dismissive. "It's not anybody at the bar. But I'm going to make sure."

He giggled at her resolve as if it were adorable.

"What? You don't think I can do it?" she said. "I'm going to find out who did this. Hear me now, believe me later."

"You're on," he said.

"And you better check your credit card balance and transactions when you get home. I have a feeling you're in for a surprise."

"I like a take-charge woman. This is going to be fun to watch—you latching onto this crime like a chihuahua on a pork chop."

"Well, somebody's got to do it," she said with a sassy head tilt.

"Touché."

CHAPTER NINE

After dinner, Brandy went to Ginny's house to pick up Hairy and to tell her all about her first date. Brandy really wanted to go down the rabbit hole on how both her credit card and Peter's credit card stopped working at about the same time. It was going to be hard to find a common denominator that would link the two crimes together—assuming Peter was telling the truth and his card had no other reason to stop working.

Brandy resolved to see if Ralph and Big Joe at the bar had any information that would help her analyze the situation. She wanted to know if they had looked at their credit card transactions and, if so, whether or not they found anything suspicious. She could then compare those suspicious charges to the suspicious charges on her own card to see if there was a recognizable pattern or if any commonalities jumped out at her.

She wanted to do the same with Peter's credit card transactions but thought better of it. They had just met. And she really liked him. She worried it would seem like she was just concocting a convenient excuse to spy on him or gather intelligence she wasn't entitled to. She was also still guarded after her break-up with Eric and was, frankly, worried about what she might find in Peter's credit card statements. She loved the idea of having someone to have cocktails with and of someone who wanted to meet Hairy and who sounded like he wouldn't even complain about how much Hairy shed on the couch or the bed. She wasn't ready to have it all evaporate as soon as she sees a charge for Victoria's Secret.

So, she decided to ask Ginny for help.

As soon as she walked into Ginny's house she yelled, "Hey Hairy! Mama's home."

Only silence answered her. She came around the corner of the kitchen into the living room to find Ginny sitting on the couch reading with Hairy laying next to her with his head in her lap. He wasn't about to sacrifice a snuggle-in-progress for the mere promise of a snuggle if he went through all the hard work of getting up.

"Nice to see you, too, ya bum," Brandy said as she patted him on the head and plopped down in a recliner.

"Sooo?" Ginny asked, setting down her book and adjusting slightly so as to face Brandy without evicting Hairy from her lap.

Brandy answered with a huge grin then opened her mouth in a silent scream and shook her head as if the world's greatest band had just taken the stage.

"I knew it," Ginny said. "I knew you were going to fall all over this guy. 'Eric who?' You were with him for two years. Don't you think you need more than forty-eight hours to unravel that whole mess before you jump into the next one?"

"Peter's not a mess. He's the opposite of a mess. He's kind and funny. He paid for dinner."

Brandy was secretly glad Ginny was skeptical. It was the perfect lead-in to her plan.

"But," Brandy said. Ginny immediately perked up at the prospect of a 'but.' "But," Brandy said again for emphasis. "I need you to do some recon for me."

"Keep going," Ginny said.

"I need you to just follow him around for a couple of days. See where he goes. Does he just go straight to work then home and back again? Or does he take some detours? I've been thinking about what you said, and I think you're right. I need to make sure he doesn't have any other women or vices I should know about before I get too invested."

Ginny was enthusiastic. "Yes. See? Now, that's being smart. That's one way you can avoid another Eric."

Brandy knew that if she asked Ginny to help investigate Peter as a means of figuring out whether he often goes anyplace she goes in order to try to pinpoint the source of the electronic pickpocketing, that Ginny would refuse to help. Ginny was sanctimonious about her own ideas of crimefighting. She loved sleuthing and she loved mysteries. But she loved to investigate sins—not crimes. She would leave the crimes to the police. Ginny was much more likely to try to catch a cheater than to catch a thief.

Brandy prayed Ginny wasn't going to catch both.

*　　*　　*

It was nearly 9:00 p.m. Eric had been texting Emily trying to get her to move back the pick-up time because the Brewers game hadn't ended yet and was tied at the top of the ninth inning. He didn't want to leave the game early just to get his wallet. She ignored him.

Finally, he texted her in frustration that he was leaving the game because he couldn't get a hold of her and she better be there with his wallet. She still ignored him.

Eric circled the neighborhood for what seemed like forever looking for a place to park. He was anxious that Emily would, again, be punching a clock and eager to leave him high and dry if he were a minute late.

Finally, he found a parking spot several blocks away. "The Cage" was in an up and coming area of the city, full of night clubs and high-end cafes. It was packed on a Saturday night—and particularly so when the Brewers were playing less than half a mile away. Baseball fans were already starting to pour out of the stadium and into the surrounding bars and restaurants.

Eric flung open the dark tinted glass door to "The Cage" and was immediately consumed by loud thumping club music and pulsing neon lights. The bar was dark but slightly illuminated by the glow of several TVs playing Madonna's "Material Girl" music video on a loop. The bright pink of the video reflected in the back-bar mirror into the crowd.

Almost as soon as Eric stepped foot in the club, a young shirtless man with coffee-colored skin and a silky black modern pompadour, threw his arm around Eric, thrusting his chiseled six-pack against Eric's side. The man leaned into Eric with pouty kissy lips and squealed, "Selfie!"

Eric tried to escape the man's aggressive friendliness.

"Do I know you?" Eric asked.

"No, but you will," the man said blowing Eric an air kiss.

As Eric recovered from the selfie-attack, he scanned the room for Emily but saw mostly men and quickly realized Emily had routed him to a gay bar. He hesitated to negotiate his way through the crowd. The men on the dance floor were trying to entice him to join them—fluttering come-hither fingers.

Instead, Eric pushed his way to the bar. He loitered there hoping to get a bartender's attention so he could describe Emily and ask if they had seen her. Eric waited uncomfortably, trying to avoid making eye-contact and willing himself to emit an unapproachable vibe. He texted Emily as he waited.

I'm here. Where R U?

No response.

Finally, the bartender acknowledged him as he sat down an enormous slushy red fishbowl in front of Eric topped with ripe ruby strawberries, fresh mint, and chocolate-dipped pineapple laced on a skewer. It looked more like an Edible Arrangement than a cocktail.

As the bartender slid Eric an oversized drink napkin and sat the mutant daiquiri in front of him, Eric tried to protest.

"This isn't mine. I didn't order this."

"It's from the lady at the end of the bar," the big-muscled, clean-shaven bartender said with a subtle nod to the opposite end of the bar. Eric followed his gaze and saw, not a lady, exactly, but a man dressed in full drag. He had a big red feathered wig, beautifully contoured makeup, and a red pleather miniskirt and matching biker-style jacket with fishnet stockings and five-inch stripper heels. He looked like a cross between Ru Paul and Reba McEntire.

He was eagerly waiting for Eric to glance over and as soon as the bartender directed his gaze, the drag-queen gave Eric a flirtatious wave.

Eric stayed at his end of the bar and while he let the gratuitous drink melt in front of him, he continued texting Emily. Twice, he even went outside to the relative quiet of the sidewalk and tried to call her to no avail. On one of those occasions, he was again accosted by the selfie-bandit, who managed to get an adorable picture of his half-naked self, Eric, and "The Cage's" neon sign illuminated in the background.

After about thirty minutes of resisting random come-ons and trying to fade into the club's darkest shadows, Emily *finally* responded.

Where am I? she texted. *I'm with Brandy comforting her. She's been crying her eyes out ever since she saw you changed your Facebook status to 'bi-curious.'*

Suddenly, it all came together for Eric. He quickly logged into his Facebook account. Shock and outrage swelled within him. He saw that his status had, indeed, been changed to "bi-curious" and staring back at him were two pictures of him and the selfie-bandit.

In that instant, he realized Emily had no intention of giving back his wallet. She had set him up! The selfie-bandit, the bartender, the drag-queen (all friends of Emily)—they were all in on the prank. And she was using his passwords to harass him.

You're not going to get away with this! he texted her furiously.

Oh, I think I will.

Eric texted Emily a string of expletives that would make one think he got paid by the word. But Emily was unaffected.

I know you stole Brandy's credit. You are a cheater and a fraud! I have PROOF. You are going to come clean to the cops or I promise by tomorrow morning you will be the most popular gay on Grindr!

You are CRAZY, he texted back. *I didn't steal anything. The only one who stole anything here is YOU. And I'm the one with PROOF now that you've been hacking into my social media accounts.*

Maybe you should just call the cops and turn me in? Like I did to you when you were driving like a maniac.

Eric was so furious, he reflexively threw his phone down, shattering the screen on the bar's painted cement floor. He swore this wasn't over. In fact, it was only beginning.

EMILY'S REVENGE

This cocktail is sweet and seductive but packs a wallop—just like Emily!

Ingredients:

1 oz Aviation Gin
.5 oz Disaronno Amaretto
.75 oz Lemon Juice
.75 oz Simple Syrup**
.5 oz Pineapple Juice
1 oz Campo Viejo Brut Cava

Preparation:

To Build Cocktail:

Mix all ingredients except Campo Viejo in shaker with ice.
Strain into cocktail glass or champagne flute and top with Cava.
Garnish with lemon twist or pineapple slice.

Notes:

This summery, pineapple upside down twist on a French 75 works well for brunch, lunch, or dinner

** To make your own simple syrup: combine 1 cup granulated white sugar and 1 cup water in saucepan over low heat. Cook, stirring often, until sugar is completely dissolved.

Remove from heat and let cool. Transfer to airtight container and store refrigerated for up to four weeks.

CHAPTER TEN

Emily called Brandy. As soon as Brandy answered the phone, all Emily said was, "You're Welcome."

"For what?" Brandy said.

"Go on Facebook and check out Eric's profile."

Brandy eagerly did as she was told. When the picture of Eric and Emily's shirtless helper loaded onto the screen, she laughed so hard, Hairy thought something was wrong and came to rest his head on her lap.

"Emily Jean West! Everyone needs a best friend like you! If we could bottle your tactics and sell them, we would be rich a hundred times over," Brandy said wiping tears of laughter from her eyes.

Emily excitedly launched into the whole story of how she had gotten Eric ticketed for not having a driver's license and had set him up to be manhandled at the gay bar.

Brandy relished every detail—except for the part where Eric threatened revenge.

"He's all bark and no bite," Emily said.

"I don't know. He can be pretty obsessive once he gets an idea in his mind. It's like with his sandwich punch cards. He becomes fixated on seeing it through."

"Well, I've dealt with the likes of Eric before. He's nothing I can't handle. Let me have my fun. And if he goes to the cops, I assume Officer Loverboy will be on our side."

"What do you mean 'our' side? I didn't even know about any of this."

"Ok. My side. But hopefully he won't hang your best friend out to dry."

"We've got Papí to protect you, too."

The Chief loved Emily almost as much as he loved Brandy, just because she was Brandy's best friend and was so loyal to her. The Chief had gotten to know Emily throughout the years at family gatherings, vacations, and holidays. The Chief would almost certainly protect Emily.

Brandy then told Emily about her date with Peter. They talked on the phone until almost midnight. Brandy also shared the concerns Peter raised with regard to the Chief and his day-drinking at "Olive or Twist." Brandy and Emily both agreed that they needed to do everything they could to help protect him and his job. It was the least they could do.

Unfortunately, while everyone at the police department seemed to know the Chief was a lush, they didn't know of all the unpaid, unacknowledged good works he quietly did for the department and the community. Each year since becoming the police chief, he had quietly donated all his sick time and personal time to other officers who had run out of leave due to new babies and family illnesses. He had also used his own personal funds when the police budget wouldn't allow for a new K-9 officer and, again, quietly arranged to anonymously donate the dog to the department. He loved his fellow officers and the community. They were his family.

And Brandy could understand why he would resist being forced into retirement. He had no wife or children of his own. He had no one to go home to at the end of the day. If he didn't have an office to go to and meetings to attend— even if it were as a mere figure head—Brandy worried he would spend not just half his days but all of his days drinking. His job at the police department offered a small semblance of routine and Brandy worried that the Chief was one of those guys who needed a purpose—and he found it in being a police officer. If that were taken away from him, he was like all those old men who died within six months of retirement because their mental health deteriorated, and their physical health followed.

Brandy and her siblings were the closest thing he had to family. Brandy suddenly felt slightly guilty that part of why the Chief was at the bar so much was to see her. He was very proud of her and her job. He patronized the bar in no small part to bask in her celebrity at "Olive or Twist," and because he wanted to take care of her. He knew that a pretty female working in a dive bar until 2:30 a.m. could be an easy target. If it was well-known that the police chief would be stopping by at any moment, it kept people on their best behavior. Or at least deterred them from behaving their worst.

After getting off the phone, Brandy still had Facebook pulled up on her computer. She decided to do a little research of her own. Not about Eric. She would leave that to Emily. Rather, she wanted to learn more about how electronic pickpockets worked so she could figure out how they might have targeted her.

Brandy had been a paralegal for many years before giving it up to diminish the stress in her life. She worked for a family lawyer who focused on divorce and child custody issues and she could never quite shake the fact she was helping rip families apart—usually for no better reason than one parent or the other decided it was better to shift their own suffering in a "loveless" marriage to their kids. So, her research skills were second to none. Friends were always amazed by how quickly she could drill-down and distill information online in order to produce, well, anything: restaurant recommendations, the perfect gif as a witty retort, the criminal background of a potential plumber or babysitter. Nothing was out of her reach.

So, she dove into everything she could find about "crowd hacking" or electronic pickpocketing. She was going to have to know as much as possible if she was going to beat these criminals at their own game.

As she researched, she made notes to reminder herself of her plan. She wanted to talk to Papí about the complaints they had been getting about credit card theft. Had they come from the same general location? Were they scattered? Did all those people have cards issued from the same bank or company? She also wanted to follow up with Ralph and Big Joe and see if they had checked their accounts and found any fraudulent charges. If so, she could look for commonalities between those fraudulent charges and the charges on her own card. It was starting to feel like a daunting task, and for a minute, she could almost understand why the police wouldn't want to undertake such a labor-intensive investigation with such little promise of a payoff. But she had to do it—for herself, for her customers, and for Papí.

*   *   *

Princess Darbie called into work Sunday night to say she wasn't going to be able to take her usual shift. That meant Brandy would have to fill-in. At least this time, Brandy had the foresight to order a pizza on her way to the bar instead of after suffering near-starvation for several hours before sneaking aside to make a call for delivery.

When she arrived at "Olive or Twist," Virgie was just ending her shift. Finn had been dropped off about thirty minutes earlier on his mom's way to work so he could go home with Virgie for the night.

Brandy was glad to see Ralph and Big Joe were still there. Finn was glad to see Hairy.

"Hairy!" he said as he hopped down from a bar stool and got in Hairy's face for a snuggle, letting Hairy lick all over his face as he giggled.

Nope. Brandy thought. *There's no way this kid is behind some big credit card scandal.*

"Hey Joe," Brandy said. "You remember a couple days ago when I ran your card and it wouldn't go through. Ralph, listen up. I'm talking to you, too. Do you guys remember that?"

"Yeah, uh huh," they both said.

"Well, did you ever check your card balances or look at your transactions online? Did you see anything suspicious on your accounts? Because I checked mine and somebody flat-out raided my account. Five thousand dollars in credit evaporated and I have all these charges now at convenience stores and grocery stores—which seems like an odd place to blow money, but all I know is it's gone."

"Is that what you were talking to that cop about the other day when he was in here?" Ralph asked.

"Yes. I was filing a police report, but it sounds like the cops aren't really going to do anything about it. They just expect the credit card company to assume responsibility and deal with it. They acted like they don't have time to investigate because it's like looking for a black cat in the dark."

"I wouldn't say this if the Chief were in here," Big Joe said, "but that sounds lazy as hell."

"Well, don't say anything, but I think they're taking cues from the Chief. They all know he spends half the day here and let's just say, while the cat's away the mice will play. They know no one is going to do anything if they half-ass an investigation. So, I'm going to find who did it myself."

"How do they know the Chief isn't here doing his own investigation?" Big Joe asked.

"Good question," Brandy said. "How do they know he's actually in here drinking? If they see his cruiser out front, he could just be in here talking to me or checking in on a neighborhood business. Is somebody in here a rat?" she yelled so everyone could hear.

"I'll be anything you want me to be, Honey. I been called worse." Brownout was sitting in his usual spot in front of the flat-screen TV.

"I'm not talking to you, Brownout. I'm just getting frustrated."

"I'd like to help you," Big Joe said, "but I don't know how to check my balance. I can look at the paper statement when it comes next month."

"Oooh! I can help," Finn said raising his hand like he was at school. "I know how to download apps."

As Finn sidled up to the men at the bar to give them a lesson in downloading banking apps, the pizza arrived.

"My hero!" Brandy swooned. "How much do I owe you?"

"Eleven dollars even."

Brandy turned her back to dig her purse out from a cubby under the bar but abruptly turned around when Virgie yelled, "Finn Patrick what is this?"

Brandy expected to see a mess of maraschino cherries and shredded orange slices strewn across the bar. Finn was famous for snacking on garnishes and leaving disaster in his wake.

But Brandy saw no mess and Finn looked startled.

"What is this?" Virgie yelped. "You charged twenty-two dollars for an 'in app purchase' for some video game I never heard of? How did you get ahold of my card?"

"I didn't," Finn said.

"Look," she said, showing him her phone. "It says right here. Who else do you know that's buying body armor and weapons upgrades for a video game?"

"Everybody. All my friends at school and . . . "

"Ok. I mean, who else do *I* know. Who else that's buying these things could have a hold of my card?"

"I don't know. Ask my mom. Every time I want to buy an upgrade, I ask her, 'mom can I spend three dollars' and she says yes or no. Then I just click the purchase button. That's all I know."

"But how is it tied to my credit card?"

"I have no idea," Finn said.

"Well stop downloading upgrades or apps or whatever you call it until I talk to your mom. I don't have twenty-two dollars every time you want to play one of your video games."

Finn shrugged her off and Virgie stared at her phone screen, exasperated.

Brandy handed the pizza guy eleven dollars plus a tip.

"Hey just a heads up," he said to Virgie. "I'm a gamer and I know what you're talking about. Those app purchases are tied to your phone or whatever account is associated with your phone number. So, if you and his mom either share a phone account or an iCloud, your card might be attached to that account. It would be the same account you pay your phone bill with every month. So, it might not be anything he or his mom specifically set up. Just something to look at. I'd hate for the kid to get in trouble for something he didn't do."

"Thanks," Virgie said. "I'll look into it. Trouble is, he's the only one smart enough to figure out how to undo it. He's a whiz with electronics. I have no idea what I'm doing."

"I didn't do it on purpose, Grandma. Sheesh," Finn said.

"Well, good luck, kid," the pizza guy said.

"Finn, do you want a piece of pizza?" Brandy asked.

"Yeah, just wait a minute 'til I'm done helping these guys."

"Well, you better help them better than you helped me," Virgie said. "Now my credit card's all messed up."

CHAPTER ELEVEN

Brandy thought she was dreaming that her phone was ringing. When she realized that reality was intruding on her sleep, she snapped her eyes open, more interested to see what time it was than who was calling.

It was almost 11:00 a.m. and it was Peter.

She swiped to answer and tried to sound chipper and alert—so he wouldn't think that he either inconvenienced her by waking her up, or that she was a bum who slept in until noon every day.

"Hey, Brandy? It's Peter."

"Yeah. Hi, Peter! How are you?"

"I'm good. I'm good. How are you?"

"Still living a dream," she joked.

"Well, I was calling to see if you're free tonight and if you wanted to grab something to eat after I get off work?"

"What time do you get off?"

"I work 7 a.m. to 7 p.m. today, so any time after 7 p.m. works for me."

"Oh, dang it! I would love to, but I had to close last night, so I asked one of my co-workers to take the opening shift today. So, I'm free until 7 p.m., but then I have to go into work. I won't get off until about 3:00 a.m. or so."

"Then what about lunch? I know it's kind of last minute, but maybe we could eat lunch somewhere?"

"That would be great!" she said.

They made plans to meet at "Blue's Egg," a popular brunch restaurant not far from "Olive or Twist."

Meanwhile, Brandy flew through her morning routine like a Tasmanian devil, trying to get ready in time. She called Ginny for some emergency help.

"Hey, can you come pick up Hairy? I'm rushing around trying to get ready to meet Peter for lunch and your place is in the opposite direction of where I'm going. I'm supposed to be there at noon."

"Ok. But while you're with him, try to see if he'll tell you what his plans are tonight. Then I can follow up and see if he's telling the truth. Also, you need to somehow get me a picture of this guy or find one online so I'm sure of who I'm dealing with. Also, find out what kind of car he drives when he's off duty."

"That's a tall order. I don't want to sound like a stalker."

"I'm sure you can find a way to work it into the conversation."

"I'll do what I can. And why don't you just google him? See if you can find a picture online. I'm sure since he's a cop he's made an appearance on their Facebook page or in the newspaper at some point."

"I did google him. Let's just say I don't have the patience or the stomach to weed through all the porn stars who use his name as their stage name."

"Ew. Really?"

"Even adding 'police officer,' doesn't narrow the search. Then it just filters down to all the male strippers with his name."

"That's hilarious. I wonder why he doesn't use a nickname?"

"Oooh. I hadn't considered that," Ginny said. "Maybe Peter Dixon isn't his real name?"

"Who would choose 'Peter Dixon' as a fake name? Who in their right mind would want to bring that on themselves?"

"Well, from the looks of it, about a gazillion strippers and porn stars."

"I'm pretty sure that's a dead-end. Just stick to the assignment. I'm less worried about his name than where he spends his time—and who he spends it with."

"Alright. I'm on it, boss."

About fifteen minutes later, Ginny arrived to dog-sit Hairy and to declare Brandy's shorts and high-heeled wedges to be inappropriate brunch attire.

"I'm trying to impress a guy, not a twenty-six-year-old piano teacher."

"Maybe try to impress him with your intelligence and your sparkling personality. Besides, your legs look really pasty." Ginny was hitting below the belt. She knew it was an observation Brandy could not rest upon.

"Arrgh!" Brandy groaned as she marched back into her bedroom. She returned a minute later in a pair of capri pants and the same shirt and heels.

"That's much better," Ginny said, though nobody asked her.

*   *   *

Ginny wasn't the only one stalking some prey. Across town, Eric had resolved to make good on his threat to get his wallet back and bring down Emily in the process. She had been ignoring his texts, so he decided to confront her at her job. He would demand his wallet and if she refused to hand it over, he would call the police—who would swarm her salon and embarrass her in front of her co-workers and *maybe* even get her fired if he could convince the cops she took the wallet intentionally.

He didn't recognize Emily's car in the parking lot outside the salon. Nonetheless, he parked outside "Curl Up & Dye" and went inside.

"Hello, can I help you?" a cheerful young receptionist said.

"Um, yeah. Is Emily West here?"

The receptionist looked at her computer and then looked slightly concerned.

"I'm sorry. She's not in yet. Do you have an appointment with her?"

"No. That's alright. Do you know what time she'll be here?"

"No. I don't. She sets her own schedule, and I don't see anything listed for her until 1:00 p.m."

"Ok. Thanks," Eric said as he left. It was close to noon. If she had a client coming at 1:00 p.m. he assumed she would be arriving soon. He decided to walk across the street to a coffee shop where he could simultaneously wait and still see the front entrance to the salon.

Once inside the coffee shop, he sat down at a two-top next to a big picture window. He scrolled through his phone and soon an employee asked him if he needed anything.

"Oh no. I'm fine," Eric said.

"Well, we have a no loitering policy. I'm going to have to ask you to buy something or leave," the employee said.

"Ah. But, that's kind of a problem. My wallet got stolen. I'm actually waiting here for somebody so I can get it back."

"I don't know what to tell you. If you aren't going to buy something, you'll need to go wait somewhere else."

"I bet if I was homeless, you'd give me coffee for free and let me sit here all day," Eric said, standing up and trying to look overpowering.

"Are you homeless?"

"No."

"Ok, then."

"Bums drink free coffee all day, but if I'm just a nice guy not bothering anybody or stinking up the place, you're going to make me leave? You're pathetic."

"Sir, please go."

Eric started walking toward the back where the bathrooms were.

"Sir, stop. You can't go back there."

"What? You're not even going to let me go to the bathroom first?"

"Those aren't for the general public. They are for paying for customers. We have a sign on the door."

Eric turned around and marched angrily back toward the front entrance of the coffee shop. As he pushed open the door, he aggressively ripped down the small hand-written sign taped to the inside of the door that declared the restrooms were for paying customers.

He walked around the corner of the strip mall where the coffee shop was located and thought about his next move as he kicked a trash can in frustration.

He also really had to pee. He couldn't go back into the coffee shop. And he couldn't go into the salon.

He shredded the confiscated door sign in anger, threw it on the ground, and then kicked the trash can again for good measure. He looked up when he heard the blip of a police siren.

A police officer had been parked in the alley along the strip mall and when he saw Eric's antics, he pulled forward and got out of the car.

This officer was slightly more amiable than the cops at Home Depot and while sympathetic to Eric's lack of I.D., still gave him a ticket for littering—with a mandatory court appearance.

Eric tried to protest, citing the trash that had overflowed the dumpster and fallen into the alleyway.

"How come you don't ticket them? They let trash fly everywhere. I just dropped one little sign and I get a ticket?"

"Well, I didn't see them put that litter there. Maybe the wind blew it. You, on the other hand, tore that sign up and intentionally threw it on the ground. If you want to try to convince the judge to believe your testimony over mine, we'll meet again at your court hearing."

Eric huffed and put his hands on his hips in defiance. He looked into the distance and saw the cheerful receptionist from "Curl Up & Dye" standing in the parking lot talking to a tow-truck driver as his pick-up was being winched onto a flatbed.

"My truck!" Eric shouted as he started to jog across the street.

"Sir," the officer yelled after him. "Are you refusing to sign your ticket? If you don't sign your ticket, I have to arrest you."

"But they're towing my car! What the hell! I wasn't even parked there for an hour and I was just talking to that girl! She knows I'm coming back!"

"Sign your ticket and you're free to go."

Eric used his thigh as a desk top and tried to scribble his name on the ticket. He nearly ruptured a vein in his forehead when the pen didn't work.

After a slow-motion search for a functioning pen, the officer finally found one. Eric quickly scrawled his name. The officer gave him his copy of the ticket and Eric took off like a shot, but it was too late. His car was already rounding the corner of the block, strapped to the tow truck.

Eric crumpled the ticket in anger and stuffed it in his pocket—out of the cop's view, of course—and ran back to the salon.

He ran into the salon in a panic and almost out of breath.

"What happened to my truck? It was parked right in front there. Why did you let them take it?" he asked the cheerful receptionist.

"Yeah. About that. We have extremely limited parking for our clients, so those stalls are for customers only. When you said you didn't have an appointment and then walked across the street to the coffee shop, I had no choice but to call a tow truck."

"Had no choice?!" he screamed. "You had me towed? I was parked there for less than an hour. Are you kidding me?" he was pacing with fury.

"We need that spot for our clients. You should have moved your car when you left. You can take it up with the city tow lot."

"Is Emily here?" he could barely utter the words.

"No. She's not."

"Ugh!" he yelled as he did an about-face. He pushed through the door so hard it nearly flew off.

*   *   *

Brandy and Peter were well into a wonderful lunch date. Brandy thought how natural it felt to talk to Peter—like she had known him forever. And she loved the attention he got in his uniform. The restaurant tried to pay for their meal as a "thank you" to Peter for his civic duties and for patronizing their business, but he wouldn't hear of it.

Brandy also insisted it was her turn to pay since he had paid for dinner at Lucky Joe's.

"Come on. Let me feel like a big shot," he said, trying to convince her to stand down.

"I just feel so weird letting you pay. I feel like I'm not doing my part."

"Don't feel like that. You did plenty by getting ready at lightning speed to meet me here. And you look very pretty," he said smiling.

Brandy immediately felt for her tooth with her tongue. Whew. It was where it should be. She could never be sure.

"Thank you," she said. "You're not so bad yourself."

Even after Peter paid the bill, they continued to loiter and chat. Neither of them wanted the date to end.

Brandy considered whether she should update Peter on the status of her investigation. She didn't want him to think she was just cozying up to him for insider information or to use him as a cheap investigation resource. She also didn't want to embarrass herself by looking like an amateur. Granted, Peter wasn't a detective, but as a police officer he certainly knew more about criminal investigations than she did. Then again, having been a family law paralegal might have been a fair equivalent. She had to constantly scrutinize text exchanges and Facebook posts and help hire and direct private investigators and review mountains of bank records. She convinced herself she wasn't a total hack.

"So, I've been doing some digging . . ." she started.

"On me?" he interrupted as he shifted in his seat.

"No, no," she laughed, knowing that was Ginny's job, not hers. "On the credit theft."

"Ohhh," he said, seeming relieved.

"I mean, I won't tell you about it if you aren't interested. I don't want to just 'talk shop.' I know how boring it would be for me to talk about beer brands."

"No. I totally want to hear about it. Let's have it," he said getting comfortable.

Brandy told Peter she was very skeptical of any implication that Finn could be the culprit. She cited his innocent demeanor, that he had no motive, that such a crime was too sophisticated for a child. Peter listened without judgment.

She also explained that she was looking for commonalities among other patrons who had their cards hacked and that she was going to analyze the transactions for a pattern.

"Better you than me," Peter said. "My eyes would glaze over if I had to look through credit card statements all day. I had the chance one time to get promoted to detective and I said, 'no thanks.'"

"Really? I think being a detective would be the best job ever!"

"I think it would be the worst! You're always on call. You have no control over your own schedule. You still have to deal with dangerous criminals. And I think it makes you jaded and skeptical. It's like they say, 'when you're a hammer, everything looks like a nail.'"

"What's that mean?"

"It means if you spend all day looking for lies, everyone looks like a liar. I wouldn't want to live like that."

"So, what do you do for fun?" Brandy asked, remembering her assignment from Ginny. "Like after work tonight? Where will you go? What will you do?"

"Well, my shift at the strip club starts at 9:00 p.m., so I'll go there next."

"What?" Brandy said, taken aback.

"Just kidding. I was just trying to make a 'Peter Dixon' joke."

"Oh, ok. I get it," Brandy said laughing.

"I don't go anywhere. My life's pretty boring. Or was until you showed up," he said with a wink.

Brandy blushed as she looked into his eyes.

"What do you do for fun?" he asked. "No. Wait. Let me guess. Roller derby?"

"Close. I used to do roller derby. But not anymore. That was years ago. It's how I lost my tooth."

"I know. The Chief told me."

"Oh no," Brandy said as she threw her head back and laughed. "I'm afraid to ask what else he might have told you."

"How about if our next date is at the roller rink?"

"Are you serious?"

"Sure. I mean, if you don't mind me looking like a complete idiot. I would love to see your roller-skating skills in action. I haven't roller skated in about thirty years. I was probably twelve or thirteen the last time I had on a pair of roller skates. I trust you'll be a patient coach. But you've gotta go easy on me."

"I'm game. I'll totally go. I haven't roller skated in years, but I think I've still got it," she said confidently.

"Ok. I'll start listening to some KISS and REO Speedwagon to get in the mood."

"Perfect. And don't forget to dust-off your limbo, while you're at it."

"Ugh. I forgot about the limbo," he groaned.

"If you're going to do this, you have to do it all the way."

"For you, I'd do anything," he said as he helped pull her chair out. They left the restaurant with firm plans for next time: roller skating or bust!

CHAPTER TWELVE

It had been several days, and Ginny had come to the bar to strategize her stalking with Brandy. Ginny didn't come to the bar often, but when she did all the regulars swooned.

Ginny was both pretty and polite and there was something about her demure appearance that made her instantly popular. She came across as buttoned-up and unapproachable and her outfits left everything to the imagination. When Ginny showed up at "Olive or Twist" she was like a hot new club and everybody wanted to be on her VIP list.

Ginny stood at the end of the bar with Hairy at her feet. Brownout rose in a chivalrous gesture and silently motioned toward his vacant stool—prime real estate in front of both the TV and the bartender, but Ginny declined with a subtle wave.

He then apparently decided to up the ante by offering her part of the bologna and butter sandwich he was eating. The bar didn't serve food, so occasionally Brownout packed a lunch.

"Oh, no. No thank you," Ginny said, waving it away.

"I can cut off the part where I already took a bite," he said, trying to sweeten the deal.

"No. I'm fine, thanks."

"If you fellas need anything, just yell. We're going to be at that table over there," Brandy said.

She and Ginny situated themselves at a table next to the front window—the only window in the bar—where they could remain mostly out of hearing range of the other customers. Sunlight shone onto the table, warming the brown faux-wood laminate top. Brandy stretched her arms across the table top to absorb the sun's warmth.

"So, I don't have much for you to go on," she said. "But I have a couple tidbits you can work with."

"Ok. I'm going to put this in the notes in my phone."

"Alright, but label it 'grocery list' or something. If anything happens to you and you get caught, I don't want any evidence."

"Wait. What are you envisioning? I was just going to park up the block from his house with a pair of binoculars—old school. And follow him if he goes anywhere and keep notes of where he goes. How can I possibly get caught? I wasn't going to peep in his windows or break into his office or anything."

"Hey, you run things your way. Whatever brings home the goods."

"Did you find out where he lives?" Ginny asked.

"No. I didn't ask."

Ginny gave a drawn-out and patronizing sigh as she started typing into her phone.

"Never mind. I'll find it," she said.

"Well, what was I supposed to do? Say, 'what's your address?' That makes me sound like a nut. Give me that," she said, grabbing Ginny's phone. Brandy quickly logged onto the state's circuit court access website where anyone with so much as a speeding ticket is outed in glorious detail.

"See? There," Brandy said as she handed the phone back to Ginny. "Anyone over forty is bound to have some kind of traffic ticket."

"Oooh! And for failing to come to a full stop at a stop sign. Are you sure you don't want me to stop right now? This guy sounds like bad news!" Ginny joked.

"Who's bad news?" Virgie asked. Brandy hadn't even noticed her come in.

"Oh nobody," Brandy said.

"Are you still talking about that Eric?" she said with disgust. Finn had arrived with her and was kneeling next to Hairy by the side door exchanging kisses.

"Oh, Virgie. I have a flyer for you. I even remembered to bring it this time," Ginny said.

"Flyer for what?" Brandy asked.

"For a painting class at the city rec department. Last time I was here, I mentioned it and Virgie said she would take it with me."

"Sounds like a blast," Brandy said in a voice that insinuated it sounded like anything but.

Meanwhile, Finn had climbed up on a bar stool and was handing out papers to Big Joe and Ralph. Brandy left Ginny and Virgie to talk about their art class while she investigated the activity at the bar.

"What do you have there, Finn?"

"Their bank stuff that you wanted."

"He tried to help us download these banking apps the other day," Ralph said, "but I said 'I don't need all that. How do I just print my statements?' So, Finn, here, he just said he'd print 'em for us."

"You gave an eleven-year-old access to your banking information?"

They stared at her blankly.

"Finn, why would you do that?" she scolded. "That's their private information. Don't they teach you about internet privacy and being safe on the web at school?"

"Yeah, but they wanted me to do it. I thought I was helping."

Then as if speaking to Finn, but in actuality preaching to the lot of them, she said, "You're not supposed to give anybody access to your personal online information—especially your banking information. It's like losing the keys to your house—anyone can find them and then anyone can just walk into your house."

"But you let me do bank stuff for the bar."

For a second, Brandy wondered whether he had a point before she realized a striking distinction.

"But I don't let you go on the bank website and do anything. I don't let you have the account numbers or passwords. I just let you write in the ledgers and calculate the math so I can make sure it matches up to the bank's records. There's a big difference," she said, though she wasn't sure if it was true.

"Then how come you get to look at their bank statements? All I did was print them off. I didn't even look at them. Besides, they're adults and they said I could." Finn was pressing the boundaries of her comparisons.

"He didn't do nothing wrong," Big Joe said. "We asked him to help. We were trying to get the information for you so we could help you catch the bad guys. Don't blame the kid."

Brandy wondered if it had hit a nerve because her credit had been stolen and she hadn't even done anything so careless as to hand her passwords over to a fifth grader. Or maybe she was reacting to a sneaking sense that Peter may have been right about Finn.

A thousand thoughts raced through Brandy's mind. What if Finn did it? What if he was stealing credit and buying video games? What if she accused him? Would it affect Virgie's willingness to keep working at the bar? What if she accused him and she was wrong? She wanted to ask Peter what would happen to a child who committed electronic pickpocketing, but she didn't want to feed into his theory or accidentally trip an investigation into Finn unless she was one-hundred percent sure he was to blame. But, who else could she ask for guidance?

"Papí!" she heard Ginny shout excitedly.

The Chief had just walked in the front door. Virgie and Ginny were still sitting and chatting in the front window. He stopped to give Ginny a big hug. Ginny was his "baby," and, in fact, he had been in Ginny's life longer than her and Brandy's real dad who passed away when Ginny was only twelve.

"Cariño!" he said, calling Ginny the equivalent of "sweetheart" or "dear one" in Spanish.

He also gave Virgie a big bear hug.

"Did I die and go to heaven? All I see are pretty ladies."

"Thank you, Honey," Brownout said in a theatrical falsetto.

"You be careful, Brownout. I almost married you right then," the Chief said.

"Brownout, did you bring me any financial statements to look at?" Brandy asked.

"Why? My card worked fine."

"No, it didn't!" Virgie corrected. "There's three things I've never seen. A leprechaun. A Unicorn. And Brownout's credit card."

"I don't trust banks. I keep all my money in cash. Under the mattress just like my daddy did during the depression."

"Then why did your daughter have to teach you how to send her money through the phone?" Brandy asked pointedly.

"Well, I keep some money in the bank, just for show. But when the Zombies come, and I gotta bugout, cash is gonna be king, baby!"

"Do you have a real bugout bag?" Finn asked Brownout.

"Of course. In it, I got a knife this long," he said holding his hands about two feet apart.

"Whoa!" Finn said, wide-eyed.

"And, let's see. I have a hand-crank radio set to the Pentagon's super-secret frequency. I can talk to any four-star general or even the President if I wanted to right now."

"Really?" Finn said in amazement.

"Oh. And astronaut food. I got plenty of that."

"Can I try some? What kind is it?"

"I got ice cream—it's freeze dried. Tastes like a dried-out sponge. You probably wouldn't like it."

"I like ice cream! Wait," Finn said, suddenly giving Brownout a skeptical look. "Do you mean an Earth astronaut or a space astronaut? Because most astronauts never even get to go into space. I want real astronaut food. Like from outer space."

As Brownout continued to entertain Finn with the details of his doomsday prepping, Brandy chatted with the Chief.

"Sooo," she sang. "I have some updates."

"I'm a step ahead of you. I hear you're going roller skating."

"Yes! But he suggested it. Not me. I'm not trying to show off. He said you told him I used to skate and now he wants to see my skills in action."

"I may or may not have said something to that effect," the Chief said, taking a slow sip of his signature Modelo.

"What else did you 'may or may not have' said about me?"

"Nothing bad. I'm on your side. I'm looking out for you."

"And I'm looking out for you, too." She watched him sit down his empty glass and raise a finger in the air, signaling her to bring another.

"Do the guys at the department know you drink in here half the day?" Brandy asked, though Peter had already told her the answer.

"Of course! It's the worst-kept secret in town!"

His sudden display of self-awareness was a surprise. Brandy got the impression from Peter that other police officers politely turned a blind eye to the Chief's drinking.

"Don't you worry that it will affect your reputation or their confidence in you? Or do they think you just drop by to see me and do actual police work?"

"Don't you worry about me, Chula," he said, using a Spanish term of endearment. "I'm not going anywhere. The guys at work. They know who I am. They know they can count on me. There's one guy, Captain Russo—he doesn't care for me. He interviewed with the mayor when I did. It came down to me and him and the mayor hired me to be the police chief. He's been looking for ways to oust me ever since. He tries to gather his little army of followers—they watch me like a hawk. But it's all good. That's all you need to know. It's all good," he said as he took another sip of his drink.

CHAPTER THIRTEEN

Armed with a basic dossier of information about Peter, Ginny was ready to commence her undercover operation. She knew from his ongoing conversations with Brandy that today he worked from 7:00 a.m. to 7:00 p.m. and then planned to go to the gym after work. Or so he said.

She staked out his house starting at 6:30 a.m. just to ensure he didn't kiss anyone goodbye at the door or escort an overnight guest to her car. Ginny was an early-to-bed, early-to-rise kind of person. So, 6:30 a.m. was nothing for her. However, she was already worried about seeing her mission through on the back end. If she had to stay awake past 9:00 p.m., it could be a problem.

Ginny took notes—detailing the things she thought were important. She approved of Peter's quaint Milwaukee bungalow. It was neatly painted, and the yard was well-kept.

The neighborhood was working-class but safe with lots of children's bikes and sun-bleached Big Wheels in the yards.

At precisely 6:45 a.m., Peter bounded out of his side door carrying a black backpack and a silver coffee tumbler.

Ok. He makes his own coffee. Nice. That means he's frugal—very practical.

She followed him to the police department, but once they arrived at the parking lot, she had to rethink her strategy. The police parking lot was restricted by an electronic arm operated by a keycard. Peter pulled in and she spent a few minutes driving around the block contemplating her next move.

After two or three loops, she was stuck at a stop light just ahead of the entrance to the police lot. A virtual convoy of police vehicles—SUVs, patrol cars, motorcycles—were leaving the lot one after the other, two even flipped on their lights and sirens as they quickly peeled away from the rest of the pack. Ginny immediately realized she couldn't possibly keep up with him during his shift—she didn't even know which car was his or if he was even part of the fleet. She hadn't learned much about how patrol cars were assigned from all her cozy-mystery reading. She also didn't know if he'd be patrolling alone or with another officer. She made an executive decision to abandon the surveillance—until 7:00 p.m.

She later decided she was grateful for the change of plans after she realized his backpack likely contained his gym clothes. She came to this conclusion after considering—but ultimately rejecting—other far more nefarious possibilities. She had not packed a gym bag on her morning trip, but she knew she was going to have to play along to get the best information.

Ginny assumed police officers didn't punch a clock. She knew that Peter had initially interviewed Brandy at "Olive or Twist" well after quittin' time, when Brandy first realized her credit was stolen. So, she didn't want to waste a whole lot of time waiting for him on the front end if she didn't have to since it was possible, if not likely, he would have to work late.

She parked adjacent to the police department parking lot at 6:30 p.m. to wait him out. Finally, at almost 7:30 p.m. he emerged. She followed him to a gym that wasn't far from the department. So far, so good. He was keeping to the schedule he had told Brandy about.

As he got out of his car, he was carrying his black backpack. Ginny grabbed her own bag and followed a safe distance behind. Ginny wasn't a gym member, but she had previously been the member of a gym on the other side of town where she did water aerobics. She asked the desk attendant if she could pay for a daily pass. It took a little extra time because she had to sit and fill out an information sheet which she was sure was going to subject her to a multitude of never-ending and unwanted mail solicitations. So, she filled it out using Brandy's information. This was Brandy's mission, after all. She should suffer the consequences of it.

After she was properly checked in, she went to the ladies' locker room to change. Ginny didn't have any "work out" clothes, so she tried to piece together a passable outfit from things she had at home based upon what she had seen other people wearing.

She wore a one-piece racer-style swimming suit over a pair of white tights. Over it all, she wore a pink sweatshirt. She wore leg warmers and tennis shoes. She looked straight out of a Jane Fonda workout video or Oliva Newton-John's

"Physical" music video, but she didn't care. She had a singular purpose: help Brandy avoid another Eric.

To this end, Ginny planned to try to flirt with Peter to see if he would take the bait. He had no idea who she was, and he was a long way off from "meeting the family," so she decided to take one for the team and do her best to tempt him into disloyalty.

After changing, Ginny found Peter picking out some dumbbells from a rack. She snuck up beside him.

"So, what size should I use?" she asked him.

"Oh, I'm sorry. I don't work here," he said.

"That's ok. I'm new. I haven't been to this gym before, and I saw your big muscles and thought surely you've been here a lot and would maybe have some advice for a newbie."

"I think when you buy a membership you get two free sessions with a trainer. That's probably the best place to start," he said, trying to excuse himself from the conversation.

"Ok, thanks," she said as she flipped her long hair over her shoulder.

He moved to an area around the corner in front of a wall-length mirror. She followed him to the same general area but set up her dumbbells a small distance from him. She had no idea how to work out with dumbbells, so she started a routine based on the song, "Head, Shoulders, Knees, and Toes."

Peter glanced over at her occasionally. She wasn't sure if he was taking the bait or if he was just casually surveying his surroundings. He would also occasionally stop to look at his phone. On one of his look-arounds she gave him a smile and fluttery wave. He looked around to see who she was waving at.

Variations of this exchange went on at different stations throughout the gym for forty minutes. Finally, Peter returned to the men's locker room. Ginny sprinted to change back into her normal clothes for fear he would beat her back to the parking lot and she would lose his trail.

To maximize her efficiency, Ginny opted to merely pull her smock dress over the swimming suit and tights. She took off only the sweatshirt and the leg warmers and raced to her car. It didn't occur to her until she had been sitting there for some time that Peter was probably taking a shower. Unlike her, he had actually worked up a sweat during his workout.

He finally got back to his car and, again, Ginny followed him. This time, he did not go straight home. He stopped off at the grocery store. Groceries were a very personal thing. They could be a window to a person's lifestyle. Ginny was excited to scrutinize his shopping. Would he be buying wine, tampons, or anything else to giveaway another woman?

Though Ginny had barely changed outfits since the gym, she thought she looked different enough to evade detection. To be sure, she quickly banded her hair into a messy top knot and, once inside, picked up a plant from the floral department to carry in front of her. She felt very smug and nearly crowned herself the Queen of Camouflage.

She followed Peter as they laced their way up and down the aisles. Peter bought cereal, beer, a big box of minute rice, some tortillas, and some bananas.

That's it? Ginny wondered. *What a bore!*

On the one hand, Ginny was happy that her minor investigation had proven uneventful. On the other hand, she was chagrined to find Peter seemed to be a completely normal and boring guy.

Ginny was happy that Peter seemed to have integrity. But, because of that, she worried about how long he would last with Brandy given her previous attraction to complicated "bad boys." Ginny was rooting for Peter and considered embellishing things a bit, just to hold Brandy's interest.

Then, while he was in the checkout line, he impulsively picked up a small spring bouquet of flowers.

Those better be for Brandy.

She trailed him all the way home and parked up the block where she had a clear view of his house. It was almost 9:00 p.m. and Ginny was getting tired. A few minutes after Peter arrived home, a pizza delivery man from "Pizza D'Action" came to the door. She had noted him texting on his phone in the grocery store and realized now he must have been ordering a pizza to catch up with him as soon as he got home. *Well, they like the same pizza place,* she thought. She could see inside Peter's house from the safety of darkness. His interior was well-lit. She saw no movement or activity aside from Peter's. It appeared he was entirely alone.

Ginny was just about to call it a night. It was almost 9:30 p.m. She started her car, but as she was getting ready to pull away from the curb, a motion light on Peter's garage lit up and his garage door started to rise.

Ah ha! I've got him. It's 9:30 at night. Where could he possibly be going? She trained her phone on the door and started filming.

Ginny watched anxiously. But no car emerged from the garage. Instead, Peter came out, wobbling on roller blades. Ginny laughed out loud to herself. She kept filming.

Peter's driveway had a steep incline and was scarred with cracks. Ginny winced as Peter hit a crack and fell forward. He slowly got up and steadied himself and tried to walk in the skates—rather than gliding on them. He got to the top of the driveway and picked up a basketball lying along the side of the house. He squared up and tried to shoot a basket into a free-standing hoop on the side of the driveway opposite the house. But as he hoisted the ball up for a free throw, the momentum of the push sent him rolling backwards. He tried to right himself by violently circling his arms but ended up overcompensating and falling on his butt.

Ginny had seen enough.

*   *   *

Brandy already knew Peter was a stand-up guy. She didn't really need Ginny to scout out his loyalty. She just needed Ginny to help establish Peter's routines to help her narrow down where he might have had his credit card hacked.

Back at "Olive or Twist," Peter was already proving his sincere interest and his loyalty. Brandy was working 7 p.m. to close, so Peter was texting her off and on to help the time pass. He checked in with her when he got off work and said he was heading for the gym.

About a half-hour later, Brandy laughed so hard she almost wet her pants when Peter innocently texted her a picture.

Get a load of this nut! he texted her. It was a candid picture of Ginny in her Fonda-wear, surreptitiously snapped at the gym.

About an hour later, he texted her again. *I seriously think this lady is following me.* He sent another candid picture of Ginny "hiding" behind a lone Easter Lily in the grocery store. He punctuated the text with three emojis: wide staring eyes, a skull, and a knife, implying to Brandy he thought she was some kind of serial killer.

Brandy texted Ginny asking how it was going, though she knew full-well the answer. Ginny boasted that she had some great counter-intelligence to share but would need a couple more days of surveillance to make sure her observations were consistent.

Well, maybe use a better disguise next time, Brandy texted her.

What do you mean? Ginny responded.

Brandy answered only by forwarding the two text messages Peter had sent her with the candid photos and serial killer emojis.

This time Ginny responded in-kind with a dozen laugh-crying emojis and a video of her own.

Peter is practicing for your date! Ginny texted.

Brandy was enamored and responded with one emoji: a single red heart.

CHAPTER FOURTEEN

Brandy was grateful it had been a slow night at the bar. She spent most of the evening playing detective. She had discovered that everything Peter told her about electronic pickpocketing was true: the police don't want to spend the resources on it if the amounts involved aren't substantial and the victims are diffuse and difficult to research. But she also learned that if enough criminal complaints come in, crime analysts can connect the dots and if there are enough victims to create a big enough crime, *then* investigative resources might be directed toward finding and prosecuting the culprit.

This gave Brandy some small relief. But she wasn't satisfied with the idea of simply building a case and then handing it over to a detective who may or may not work it up. If she was going to do the leg work, she was going to make sure the criminal was caught, and she was going to make sure she got the credit—no pun intended.

Brandy educated herself enough about electronic pickpocketing that she felt fairly confident starting with a few basic filters. First, she wanted to figure out whether the victims had credit cards with RFID (Radio Frequency Identification) or if they merely had the card numbers embedded on electronic strips on the back of the cards. Cards with RFID technology were more obscure because the technology was becoming outdated, but those cards were susceptible to crowd-hacking. They could be secretly skimmed through the air using radio waves that merely scanned for the cards' frequencies. Cards with electronic strips—and that did not emit a radio frequency—had to be physically connected to a skimmer to be stolen. The card had to be inserted into a modified scanner at a point of sale. Either kind of skimmer—via radio frequency or via hardware—required a high degree of technological sophistication. But, if all the victim-cards were of one class or another, Brandy could quickly determine whether the scanner was remote or whether it was actually wired to a fixed location.

Brandy had gone through both Ralph and Big Joe's credit card statements along side her own. She had eliminated Ralph as a victim. Even though his card had many unusual and diverse transactions, he claimed them all: from the phone calls to Japan to the airline tickets to Brussels, Belgium. He could account for them all. Brandy's card, on the other hand, had many unauthorized transactions—mostly at grocery stores and convenience stores.

At first, she had asked Papí if he could help her get surveillance videos from the stores where her transactions were made. If she could simply see who was standing at the counter when the transactions went through, it would be a slam dunk. But Papí told her obtaining the videos would be impossible without a subpoena or search warrant—neither of which could be obtained unless a prosecutor authorized them.

Brandy was disheartened and felt like she was trapped in a Catch 22: she couldn't get the footage without a cooperative prosecutor, but a prosecutor would be unwilling to cooperate without corroborating evidence.

However, the issue became moot when she realized the transactions on her statement were coded for online purchases. When she told this to Papí, he suggested the culprits were probably buying gift cards.

"That's how these criminals work," he told her. "They use your card to buy prepaid gift cards because those can be used anonymously. It would be too easy to track them if they were using your card to buy things on Amazon. Then we could just follow the shipping trail straight to their door. They're much smarter than that. Prepaid VISA cards can't be traced to any particular person."

"Eric had $400 in prepaid VISAs in his wallet when Emily took it," Brandy said with concern.

"You mean when she found it," he said with a wink, proving he had Emily's back.

"Yeah. When she found it. And he had that credit card in his wallet with my name on it, too. But I don't think he was lying when he told Peter it was mine and he accidentally picked it up. He didn't protest giving it back. And when I looked up the card on line, absolutely nothing had been charged on it in over four months. I mean, I'd love it if it was him. If he could sit in jail, nothing would make me happier. But I don't think he could do something like that. Could he?"

"There's an easy way to find out. I'll send Peter over to ask him. Peter will know if Eric's lying or not. And he knows how to tee up an investigation. You know, I tried to make him a detective once."

"Yeah. He told me. I wish he would have taken it. It would be so cool to be dating a detective."

"So, you are officially 'dating' now?" he said with a sly grin.

"I don't know. I'd say so."

"Well, let me send Peter to have another little talk with Eric."

"Ok. It's just so weird—having my new boyfriend investigate my old boyfriend. Isn't that some kind of conflict of interest or something?"

"What other choice is there? This is West Allis. If I had a rule that my guys couldn't investigate crimes involving their friends or family members, there would be no one left to investigate anything."

"True. I guess everybody knows everybody around here. Do you think you could do me one more favor?"

"Anything for my girl."

"Can you take a look at the other complaints that have come in recently—you said a lot of people had been calling in to report their credit had been stolen. Can you find out two things for me? First, I need to know what bank those cards are from. Second, I need to know if those cards have a little wi-fi symbol on the back or if they just have a plain old electronic strip."

"I'll get you what you need. But don't let anybody know. I wouldn't want to ruin my reputation as a loveable lush by doing any actual police work," he said with a wink.

"Your secret's safe with me."

*   *   *

After a discreet side bar with the Chief, Brandy turned her attention back to her other customers.

Ralph almost seemed disappointed that he wasn't among the credit theft victims. He was lamenting how the thieves could favor Big Joe as a victim over him—asking Big Joe how much credit he had on his card and declaring that it wasn't enough to bother with when Ralph had so much more.

"Girls, girls, you're both pretty," Brownout said. "It ain't a competition. If you want, I'll steal your card, Ralph. Then you can be part of the in-crowd."

They all laughed at themselves.

"Hey, Brownout. I heard you telling Finn about your hand-crank radio to the Pentagon. You should bring that in some time. I've heard about those crank-radios, but I've never seen one in my life. How do they work? I bet Finn would really get a kick out of seeing one."

"Oh, it's nothing fancy. Nothing like kids have now. He's seen way better electronics."

"Well, bring it in. That's an order," Brandy said. "I want to see it and I think Finn would like to see it. If you're going to talk the talk about your direct line to the Pentagon, you better walk the walk."

"Aye aye, Captain," he said giving her a salute. "But I don't know if it will work in here. It's pretty dark and you don't have any windows."

"I thought those things were supposed to work in underground survival bunkers," she said.

"Maybe so. I ain't never tried it."

The front door of the bar opened and as soon as she saw the silhouette against the glare of the afternoon sun, she immediately scooped Brownout's bologna sandwich onto the floor. Hairy sprung to action and started wolfing it down at

Brandy's feet. She knew Hairy wouldn't move an inch if he thought bologna sandwiches were going to rain upon him.

It was James Fraley, health inspector.

Brownout didn't protest Brandy using his sandwich as a decoy to keep Hairy still. He was an ally all the way. Meanwhile, Brandy's mind raced about how to get Hairy outside or upstairs. As James approached the bar, all she could hear was Hairy's juicy smacking and gulping. She turned up the volume on the TV.

"Hi Brandy," James said looking around the bar.

"Hi James. What brings you in today? I thought you already did your inspection for the month. Are you still looking for your tablet?"

"No. No," he said seeming a little uneasy and still looking around the bar. "Hey, do you happen to have a computer I can plug into? I need to charge my phone. It's on its last legs and I forgot to bring the AC adapter and I don't want to have to sit in my car. It's too hot. If you have a computer I can plug into, it should only take about fifteen minutes."

"Um, sure," Brandy said. It seemed like an unusual request, but it was going to buy her just enough time to sneak Hairy out without James seeing him. She positioned herself in front of Hairy so that he couldn't be seen from around the open end of the bar and motioned toward the back office.

"It's in the office," she said.

"Thanks."

As James' back was to the bar and he was walking down the hallway, Brandy and the bar-goers flew into mission-mode. Brandy, Brownout, and Ralph started communicating with a series of hand signals that rivaled SEAL Team Six. Brandy reached down to tug at Hairy's collar so she could escort him around the corner of the bar and to the door, but he wasn't quite finished with his sandwich and gave her a menacing growl in warning.

More hand signals ensued, and Brandy quickly reached into the under-counter refrigerator and extracted a canned pineapple ring from a Tupperware container. She flashed it at Hairy who immediately flinched. He abandoned his remaining Sandwich From Heaven and, without taking his eyes off the pineapple ring, slunk along the side of the interior shelving under the bar.

Hairy was irrationally mistrusting of pineapples—a fear Brandy could not explain. But the phobia was engrained and reliable to such an extent any presentation of a pineapple would cause him to drop everything and scout for safety.

In a matter of seconds and without saying a word, Brandy had chased Hairy away from the sandwich with the pineapple and handed Ralph a dog leash. He escorted Hairy around the bar and out the side door. Through secret hand gestures, they had negotiated a walk up and down the block until Brandy could text Ralph that the coast was clear.

James returned from the back office and sat on a barstool at the end of the bar none the wiser.

"Come on over. I don't bite," Brownout said, inviting James to move toward the middle of the bar in front of the TV.

"I'm fine, thanks."

Brandy offered him a drink, which he declined, and he sat there awkwardly with no phone to scroll through. He rested his elbows up on the bar, hands clasped, and watched Brandy. Finally, he just blurted it out.

"So, is that your sister's car out front?"

"Ginny? Yeah, it is."

"Is she here? Or is she stopping by sometime today?"

Aaaah! I get it now! Brandy saw where this was going.

"No. We actually switched cars today because I have a weird schedule, and I need an oil change. So, she said she'd take my car in for me today. Were you hoping to run into her?" Brandy said pointedly.

"Oh. Well, I mean," James started to stammer. Brandy was very direct, and he seemed taken aback by her calling him out.

She understood now why he had been stopping by at odd times without any real reason. For a split-second, Brandy envisioned a world where Ginny and James were madly in love and it no longer mattered if Hairy was in the bar. He would kindly overlook it out of loyalty to his lady-love. But, just as quickly, she envisioned his vengefulness and him shutting the bar down as soon as Ginny broke his heart. She didn't know James well at all aside from his professional role. She had no idea what he was like as a person.

"So, what's her situation?" James finally asked.

"Are you into Amish women?" Brandy said stoically.

"Oh," James said with surprise. "I didn't know. She's Amish?"

"She can build a barn in six hours—while simultaneously canning forty-eight jars of rhubarb jelly."

James looked stricken. Then Brandy started laughing and he suddenly relaxed—looking slightly embarrassed that he had actually believed her for a second.

"So . . . her situation . . ." Brandy hesitated. Was he a stalker? After all, he knew what her car looked like and he had been stopping in the bar randomly trying to just "happen" into her. Then again, West Allis was small. Everybody knew everybody. It was entirely likely he hadn't just seen her at the bar. He could have seen her anywhere. She decided to be honest and, if it came down to it, to let Ginny decide if she wanted to take a chance on him or not.

And although Ginny had never had a real boyfriend, James looked like he might be her type. He looked to be about thirty years old with feathered hair and a full but close-cut beard and mustache. He wore a lot of short-sleeved dress shirts. Brandy pegged him as the kind of guy who drove the speed limit and said things like "fifty-five, stay alive" and liked to go to breakfast after church.

It was hard not to "big-sister" Ginny by trying to protect her from a bad experience. But she also knew that if the tables were turned and Ginny had unilaterally decided the guy asking about her wasn't good enough, she would be insulted and angry. And who was Brandy to say? Maybe James was Ginny's perfect match?

"She's single," Brandy answered.

James smiled ear to ear. "Really? I don't want to do anything weird like ask you for her number. I don't want to put you in that position. But, maybe—would you be willing to just shoot me a text the next time she stops in?"

He had redeemed himself as a potential stalker by at least trying to not come across as creepy and showing a little bit of self-awareness.

"I could do that," Brandy said.

James seemed to relax and smiled happily. He moved closer to Brownout and started to chat with him.

Brandy texted Ralph. "Sorry Ralph, looks like it's going to be a while."

CHAPTER FIFTEEN

It was the night of the big roller-skating date. It was a little after 8:30 p.m. when Peter picked up Brandy. West Allis had a small-town throw-back to the roller rinks of the 70's called "Rink-E-Dink."

As they drove to the rink, Peter gave Brandy an update so they could enjoy the night without "work" hanging over his head.

He had met again with Eric at the Chief's request to question him about the prepaid VISA cards Emily "found" in his wallet.

"And I hate to say it, but it all checks out," Peter said.

"Really? So, what's the story. Why does he have all those VISAs?"

"I asked him. I told him we were still investigating your credit theft case and that we had determined your card had been used to buy a bunch of prepaid gift cards . . ."

"*I* had determined," she interrupted.

Peter smirked. "Yes, *you* had determined someone bough a bunch of gift cards with your credit cards and we learned he also had a stash of prepaid gift cards. He wanted to know how I knew that he had a bunch of gift cards.

"I told him that we had interviewed Emily West and she had stated he had them in his wallet. Well, at that point, he launched into a big bitter tirade about how Emily still had his wallet and wouldn't give it back and how she better not use those VISA cards, they belong to him. Did he and Emily not get along or something?"

"It's complicated," Brandy said. "Go on."

"Well, anyway, he wanted me to arrest her for stealing his wallet, blah blah blah. Finally, I was able to get him back on track. I asked him how he got those gift cards or why he had so many of them. He said that his customers sometimes pay him in prepaid VISA cards. Is that true?"

"I have no idea. I mean, his business is kind of shady. I guess anything's possible."

"I definitely got that impression. He told me the names of the customers who had recently paid him with VISA cards. I actually followed up with them and they corroborated his story."

"His clients are as bad as he is, though. I don't know if you can just take their word for it."

"I didn't. I made them prove they bought those cards. I talked to two different clients, and both of them were able to give me either receipts or their own credit card statements that matched up."

Brandy sat in silence taking it all in.

"I'm the last guy who wants to give Eric any credit, but I think he's telling the truth. I don't think he stole your credit or used your card to buy a bunch of prepaid VISAs. Is it a questionable business practice? Yes. Is it proof of criminal activity? No."

"Huh," Brandy said.

"And you might tell Emily to just give the guy his wallet back. He was telling me all kinds of stuff about how she's been trying to sabotage him. If it's true, I have to tip my hat to Emily. But, if she's intentionally withholding his property without his consent, she's inching toward a misdemeanor."

Brandy couldn't decide if she was happy or mad that Eric wasn't the culprit. She also couldn't decide if she was happy or upset that Peter admonished her to get Emily under control. She was happy that he was a good cop and a rule-follower. But she was slightly annoyed to learn Emily probably wasn't going to get a whole lot of leeway. At least she still had Papí as her always-and-forever trump card.

They arrived at the roller rink. Walking through the automated doors was like walking through a time-travel portal. The dark carpet glowed with a confetti-like pattern that illuminated under the black lights over the snack bar area. They walked to an area of narrow wooden benches and beige metal mini-lockers where they could change into the skates they brought.

Peter tried to downplay his inline stakes. They were old. He hardly ever used them. He was probably going to break an ankle. But Brandy knew from Ginny's surveillance he had been practicing for tonight.

Brandy still had a pair of her old roller-derby skates. They were something she kept more as a memento of her experiences than as a practical matter. She hadn't actually worn them in years.

They shoved their jackets, shoes, and Brandy's purse into a locker and Brandy slipped the springy plastic coil key-holder around her wrist. She offered Peter a helpful hand. He grabbed it with a look of, "here we go!"

He tried to walk—almost in a marching motion—across the sticky carpet, holding onto Brandy's hand for balance. They made it to the rim of the rink and Brandy crossed the threshold first—like a parent taking the first jump into a chilly pool. She turned around backward and held out both hands.

"Come on," she said encouragingly.

Peter tepidly stepped one skate onto the rink and reached for Brandy's hands. He then stepped with the other skate. Brandy skated backwards while helping steady Peter, who was facing her.

"You're doing it!" she said. "Nice job!"

He was slowly starting to abandon his "marching" and was trying to actually glide on the skates.

Pulsing lights and a large disco ball above the center of the rink fluttered around the dim skating area. Boston's "More than a Feeling" was playing over the PA.

A teenage boy skated up to them wearing a "Rink-E-Dink" t-shirt and a referee's whistle around his neck. He needed to check their skates to make sure they were "rink sanctioned" since they brought theirs in and hadn't rented them on site. Brandy held onto Peter's hands as he balanced on each leg in turn, lifting the other one slightly for the boy's inspection. After both of them passed, the boy signaled his approval with a quick two tweets of his whistle and then waved his arm with a flourish as if inviting them to pass over an enchanted bridge.

Brandy and Peter laughed at the boy.

"That would have been my dream-job when I was fifteen," Peter said. "Where else can a kid get that kind of power and authority?"

"My dream job was to be a judge," Brandy said. "But when I got older and realized you had to first go to college and then to law school and then work as a lawyer for many years and then get involved in politics, I got lazy and only went to paralegal school."

"Paralegal school isn't lazy."

"True, I guess I only saved myself one year of education by going that route." Brandy had a four-year degree in legal studies from a local state college and a two-year paralegal certificate from a community college. "After seeing it up close, I wouldn't want to be a lawyer. It's too much responsibility."

"You strike me as someone very responsible. Very take-charge. Like you would let nothing get in the way of getting what you want."

"That's probably true in some respects," she said. "You *don't* strike me as someone who was power-hungry when he was fifteen."

"Nah. I would have only had a job like this to impress the ladies," he joked. "How much am I impressing you now?" He continued to wobble and skate unsteadily while tightly gripping Brandy's hands.

"For your skating, I'd give you a two. For your company, I'd give you a ten."

They made a slow and deliberate loop around the rink before Peter was ready to let go and try a loop untethered to Brandy.

"Don't wait for me," he said. "Take a lap. Let's see what you've got!"

Brandy took a spin while Ace Frehley's "Back in the New York Groove" provided a soundtrack. Peter barely moved but kept his eyes on her the entire time. As she finished her lap, she slowed next to him and he reached out and grabbed her around the waist. Brandy looked pleasantly surprised.

"Like this," he said, wrapping one arm around her waist. "This will give us a better center of gravity."

"Oh, ok," Brandy said sarcastically in acknowledgement of his little ploy to put his arm around her.

They did a couples' skate, side-by-side, with their arms around each other. Peter was getting more comfortable on his feet and was gliding intentionally instead of due only to Brandy's momentum.

An announcement came over the loud-speaker for everyone to line up for a speed-skating contest.

"What is that?" Peter asked as Brandy tried to steer them off the rink.

"They line you up and then you sprint on your skates to the wall and back. Sometimes they'll do it as a relay, but this one is just an individual race."

"I want to do it," he announced.

"Are you serious?" Brandy asked.

"Sure. Why not?"

"Because you might die," she said as she laughed. "Those ten-year-olds will eat you alive!"

"I think I can take'em," he said. "In fact, how about this? If I win, you have to give me a kiss."

Brandy was slightly disappointed. Any kiss contingent on Peter winning a skating race had no chance of happening.

"Ok. You're on," she said as she secretly resolved to kiss him anyway—just for being brave enough to humiliate himself in front of her.

The fifteen-year-old called entrants to the line. People of all ages lined up—moms, dads, little kids, teenagers. It was anybody's game. The referee lined everybody up and gave a quick overview of the rules: no pushing, no horseplay, no grabbing other racers. They had to skate to the opposite wall, touch it—where another referee would be judging the touches—and race back. First three finishers across the line would win a prize.

Peter clapped and rubbed his hands together as he looked over to Brandy for approval. He was really getting into it. She was impressed by his moxie.

The referee scrutinized the imaginary starting line to ensure no one's toe was over the line. When he was satisfied, he waited a beat and then tweeted his whistle. Everyone took off like a flash. Including Peter. He was suddenly sure on his feet and raced as if he had been skating his whole life.

Brandy was aghast. She yelled and cheered as Peter quickly pulled ahead of the pack. Staying low, he plowed to the back wall, and in one deft move, touched it, spun around, and pushed off of it all at the same time.

Who is this guy? Brandy thought. She couldn't believe her eyes. Then, as he was racing back, she could see his grin and she knew immediately what had happened.

He easily won the race and after receiving a voucher good for two free skate passes, he glided over to Brandy who was resting her elbows on the waist-high barrier wall.

"I don't know how to skate! Help me! Hold my hands! Let me put my arm around you!" she said in a fake whiny voice pretending to be Peter. "You're a fraud!" she said laughing.

"Busted," he said with a sheepish grin as he put his arm around her.

"You really played that to the hilt," she said. "Nicely done. I honestly believed you were a beginner."

"I just wanted to hold your hands and have an excuse to put my arms around you."

"You don't need an excuse for that." She spun around on her skates to face him, gripped his shoulders and gave him a sweet kiss on the lips. When she looked him in the eyes, he was grinning from ear to ear. "That's because I like you. Not because you earned it. You cheated! You knew you were going to win that race!" She laughed again at how well he had foiled her.

"I played hockey as a kid—for almost ten years. I'm not as graceful as you are on roller skates, but I can hold my own. They aren't much different from ice skates."

"I'm not in for any more surprises, am I? You haven't just been pretending to be a cop? You're not married with four kids?"

"Nope. No more surprises. I swear. What you see is what you get."

She pretended to stand back and size him up. She looked him up and down and then cocked her head to the side.

"You'll do."

CHAPTER SIXTEEN

It was a little after 10:00 a.m. Brandy was scheduled for the opening shift. But when she and Hairy arrived early, Brownout was already there with his bicycle propped against the side of the building. He stood with his back against the brick wall, holding a dusty green box under one arm while he tried to scroll through his phone.

"Isn't Virgie working today? I brought something for Finn."

"She should be in around 11:00 a.m. I just came to open up. What do you have?"

"I got my crank radio that you wanted to see." He took the green box from under his arm and held it out to her.

"Oooh! Fun. Finn's going to love it. When I'm done with my chore list, I want you to show me how it works."

Brandy unlocked the doors and ushered Brownout and Hairy inside. She poured Brownout his triple rail vodka over extra ice.

"You're in charge, Brownout. I've gotta run in the back for a minute to get Hairy some food."

"That's like the fox watching the hen house!"

"Do I need to mark my bottles like a parent trying to catch a teenager? You keep your hands off the well," she teasingly scolded.

She went to the back office where she kept a secret stash of dog food for Hairy. She had cans of it inside the desk drawer with the labels torn off. That way they would be unidentifiable if James Fraley ever saw them. But as she bent down to open the drawer, she noticed the stack of bank statements she had been researching was gone.

Brandy had taken Ralph and Big Joe's bank statements and had been comparing them along side her own whenever she had a spare minute at work. She had left them organized in a pile on the corner of the desk next to the laptop. She was going to further compare them to the information the Chief was gathering for her from other credit theft victims to look for patterns. She knew she wouldn't have tossed them out.

She immediately called Matt, her co-worker and assistant manager. She asked if he had seen the bank statements on the corner of the desk. He claimed ignorance and said he hadn't been in the office for days. Matt didn't handle many of the bar's administrative tasks. She had never known him to get on the bar's laptop or snoop through the records and she didn't actually suspect him of any wrongdoing. She wondered simply if he had any knowledge of their whereabouts.

She pressed him on whether or not he had let anyone else into the back office. He claimed he hadn't, and he denied seeing anyone go back there. The only other person who ever had any business in the back office was Chaz and he didn't actually *do* anything in there. He mostly just hid out while he made his monthly appearance until he had logged enough time in there to justifiably end his visit.

Brandy dug through the drawers. She looked in the trash. She looked under the desk. The bank statements were nowhere to be found.

She suddenly recalled James' Fraley's odd request to plug his phone into her computer. He wouldn't have taken them. Would he?

Brandy fed Hairy, handed Brownout the TV remote, and immediately called Ginny.

"Hey. I have another mission for you."

"Oh good, because I'm ready to give you my report on Peter. It's only two words long: bo-ring."

"It's not about Peter. I have another lead. But it has to do with my credit theft."

"Are you still on that kick? It's been, like, two weeks. Just cancel your card already. You're not responsible for the charges. Move on with your life and let the cops handle it."

"That's the problem, Ginny. They're not handling it. And they're not going to handle it—for me or for anyone else who comes along. It's too small-time. But it's big to me. And it's big to Papí. I think his job might be at risk."

Ginny was confused. "What does that have to do with your credit theft? And why do you think that? Like, do you think he could get fired? What happened?"

"All I know is that Peter said the department has been trying to force him to retire because he's an embarrassment to the force. They think he just sits in the bar and drinks and doesn't do anything."

"Well that's not true," Ginny interrupted.

"I know it's not, but nobody else knows him like we do. I brought it up to Papí and he was dismissive. He said that some guy who got looked over for the police chief job is just bitter and has it out for him. Papí said it's all good. That he's not going anywhere. But you know how he is. He wouldn't say anything if he thought it would worry us."

"Okay. But what can we do about it? And what does this have to do with your credit card theft?"

"Papí had told me that these cases are almost impossible to solve. He said if he could solve just one electronic pickpocketing case he'd look like a hero and other departments would be begging to know how he did it. So, we need to find out who did this—for me and for anyone else who was victimized, so the culprits will know they CAN be caught, it's not too hard to solve. But also, for Papí, so he can get the credit he deserves."

Ginny took a deep breath and sighed.

"Come on, Ginny. I need you to help me."

"Well, what do you want me to do now?"

"I want you to go out with the health inspector."

"The health inspector?" Ginny shrieked. "Why?"

"Because he was in here asking about you. But also, because I think he may have stolen some of my evidence."

"Why would I want to go out with him if he's some kind of thief?"

"So, you can help me catch him. Jeez!"

There was a long silent pause. "Well, is he cute?"

"Does it matter? I just need to you do some sleuthing. Don't focus on the date. Focus on getting the goods."

"What did he ask about me?"

"He recognized your car out front and then came in acting all weird. He asked if he could use my computer to charge his phone, then he sat there and proceeded to ask if you were going to be stopping by and what your situation is."

"Really?" Ginny cooed, clearly flattered.

"At first, I thought he just wanted to charge his phone as an excuse to sit there for fifteen minutes to see if you would come in and to ask about you. But, today, when I went into the office, I noticed a stack of bank statements is missing. The only people who have been in there are me and him. I'm worried that he took them and if he did, I need to know why. I also need to know if he was really charging his phone or if he was somehow downloading stuff from that computer."

"Well, I can't do all that! I don't know anything about computers," Ginny said.

"I wasn't asking you to. I was just thinking out loud and telling you what all I need to investigate and why I need help. So, will you do it? Pleassssse."

"What's in it for me?" Ginny asked, doing her best little sister impression.

"A swell of pride in having helped your sister and your fellow man and Papí."

"I know. But what's in it for me? I'm all for saving Papí's job and helping you do it. But you're sending me into the lion's den. I don't even know this guy. Ask Virgie, he could try to kill me."

"Virgie doesn't exactly have the most objective standards of reasonableness."

"Then you go out with him," Ginny said.

"No! I can't. I'm dating Peter! Besides, he doesn't want to go on a date with me, he wants to go on a date with you."

"Can't you just ask him if he took the papers?"

"No. Because if I'm wrong, I look like a flake for accusing him and this guy holds my bar in the palm of his hand. I can't afford to get on his bad side. And if he *did* do it, I don't want to tip him off by asking. He'll just deny it and then I'm stuck. You can get the goods a lot more effectively."

Ginny was quiet. Thinking about the proposition. Finally, she spoke.

"I'll do it, but you have to mow my lawn."

"Are you kidding me? Your lawn is the worst!" Brandy was indignant, but Ginny was dead serious. She lived in what had been their childhood home. After their father died and after Ginny was grown, their mother moved to Arizona for the warmer climate. She would be returning in a few weeks to spend the summer in Milwaukee as she did each year to escape the worst of the Arizona heat. She stayed with Ginny, and in exchange for free room and board the rest of the year, Ginny was obligated to maintain the home—and yard—in all its original glory.

Their father had a green thumb like Brandy, and he spent years lovingly cultivating an extremely well-manicured and expertly landscaped yard. But it was excruciating to maintain. The front yard was a nearly forty-five degree incline up to the house that sat on a tidy little hill. The back yard was a hazard of landscaping pavers, brick trim ledges, and a koi pond. It also was home to various fruit trees, so mowing required a scrutinous picking-up of dropped cherries and crabapples.

"You mow, or I say, 'no,'" Ginny said. Now Brandy was silent on the other end.

"Ok. But only because Mom's coming, and I want it to look nice for her."

"Hey, whatever gets your sweet cheeks over here."

With the deal negotiated, Brandy wanted to get down to business. "Ok," she said. "I have a plan for how this is going to go down. James—that's his name—he asked if I would text him the next time you come to the bar. So, all you have to do is come to the bar. I'll take it from there."

"Fine," Ginny said with pained resignation.

Brandy went back out to the front bar where Brownout was still nursing his beer and sitting next to his radio.

"So, let's rev that sucker up," she said.

"Isn't Finn coming? I thought you wanted him to see it."

"I don't know. Virgie should be here any minute. We'll see if he's with her." Brandy granted Brownout a slight time delay while she finished her morning tasks. She was outside watering the flowers when Virgie and Finn pulled up.

"Finn! Brownout's here. He has a surprise for you!"

"Did he bring me astronaut food?"

"I don't think so. He brought his radio that he said can call the President."

"Do you think we can call the President today?"

"Go in and ask him," she said.

Brandy greeted Virgie and they spent a minute admiring Brandy's gardening skills before they went inside. Finn was already up on a bar stool invading Brownout's personal space as he kneeled up high and leaned over the radio that was positioned on the bar.

"It's gotta be set up just right or it won't get a signal," Brownout said.

"Hey, Finn," Brandy said while Brownout futzed with the radio to position it just right. "You didn't happen to take those bank statements you gave me, did you? They were on the desk in the back office and now I can't find them."

"No. I didn't take anything."

"Because if you felt like you got in trouble from me for having them and wanted to get rid of them, I wouldn't be mad. I just need to know what happened to them."

"I don't have them," he said, still focused on the radio.

"Do you promise? Cross your heart, hope to die?"

"Yess," he said as he turned to hiss at her with wide eyes.

"Ok, sheesh!" Brandy said.

"Did you make this radio?" Finn asked Brownout. "It looks old."

"I didn't make it, but I did set it up so that when the government gives the word, I'll be dialed into their frequency to await instructions."

"What do you know about radio frequencies?" Brandy asked Brownout.

"Enough," he said with a smug grin.

"How do you know what frequency to set it at and how do you actually set it at the right frequency? What happens if you set it to the wrong frequency? Can it interfere with other radio waves?"

"That's top secret," Brownout said with a nudge to Finn. "And that's a lot of questions. I can't even remember them all."

Brandy had both her debit card and her credit card in her hand. As Brownout explained the radio to Finn, she discreetly put the cards on the bar next to the radio and stood there as if she, too, were listening to his explanation.

Brownout showed Finn how to crank it to life and told him how much battery power he could expect once it was fully cranked. Finally, Brownout started turning dials, looking for a frequency that would produce an audible broadcast. From Brandy's vantage point, it looked like Brownout's radio was nothing more than an amateur crank radio that anybody could figure out how to use.

Her suspicions were confirmed when she learned the radio was not actually tuned to the Pentagon or to any super-secret direct line to the President. Rather, Brownout had it tuned to some conspiracy theory radio show that promised to transmit the "Pentagon's frequency" in the event of a national threat.

It appeared Brownout was all bark and no bite. While he may have had an interest in dabbling in electronics and seemed to have some minor insight into how banking apps worked thanks to his "good for nothing daughter," he did not seem to have any meaningful technological sophistication whatsoever. At least not to the level needed to engineer and use a radio-controlled credit card skimmer.

It seemed his hesitancy to bring the radio in and his premature excuses about how it might not work properly in the bar were just defensive reactions to being outed as nothing more than an inept hobbyist once someone realized he really didn't have a direct line to the President.

Still, Finn was impressed. Brownout would always have one fan in his corner.

CHAPTER SEVENTEEN

Brandy decided to double-down on her suspicions about James Fraley. The more she thought about it, the more she started to convince herself he was up to no good. He had unfettered access to the bar—and almost every other bar and restaurant on the east side of town. He had a tablet and fancy little temperature readers—any of them could have been discreetly modified to wirelessly skim credit cards. But the real concern was that those bank statements went missing right after he charged his phone with her computer.

Brandy began to wonder if she was treading on dangerous ground. She considered whether she should tell Peter about James Fraley, but then thought better of it when she decided she would sound as bad as Virgie or Brownout with their pessimistic and overblown theories about everything.

So, she called Caroline for help.

"Hey, girl. It's me," Brandy said. "I need to pick your brain about something."

Brandy told her all about how her credit had been stolen and that the police were impotent investigators, so she had taken matters into her own hands and *maybe* had identified the culprit . . . but she needed to know if anyone had downloaded anything from the bar's laptop.

"He and I were the only ones who had been in there and I just think it's weird that he asked to charge his phone through the computer. I mean, who does that? He gave me some excuse about it being too hot in the car and I was distracted trying to hide Hairy, so I didn't make a big deal about it. But now those bank records are gone, and I can't shake the feeling he might have stolen stuff from the work computer. So, is there a way to figure that out? I know you have the inside scoop on how to track people."

"Just Danny," Caroline quipped.

"Yeah," Brandy said. "So, I thought maybe you could point me in the right direction. Because if he did take anything off the computer, I can spare my sister a fake date with a felon. And I swear to God if he stole anything—those bank records, computer files—and then had the nerve to act interested in Ginny as some cover up, so help me God . . ."

"Oh, I've seen God helping you. Remember? I was there when the firefighter started swinging that ax!"

They both laughed and then commiserated a bit as Brandy told Caroline about the aftermath of her break-up with Eric—how Emily had taken it upon herself to exact revenge and how the universe had rewarded Brandy with a new boyfriend.

Caroline was ecstatic about the update in all respects.

"But back to the computer," Brandy said. "Can you help? What should I do?"

"My dear, sweet, Brandy," Caroline said in a low soothing voice like Maleficent. "Of course, I can help you. I have this software. I call it my 'cheater beater.' You install it on your computer, and it will run a report of all the keystrokes that have been entered—it can recreate emails, banking passwords, direct messages on Tinder—you name it. So, if someone got on your computer and typed anything on the keyboard, it will show up."

"So, how do I get this software?"

"Oh, I have it on a flash drive. Are you at 'Olive or Twist?' I'll bring it over and run it for you."

"Would you?" Brandy squealed. "Oh, thank you thank you thank you. You're the best!"

Caroline arrived with Danny in tow, of course. They had been to the bar many times to see Brandy, so Danny was happy to occupy a barstool with Ralph and Big Joe. He couldn't help but wonder if he was seeing his future—sitting in a dive bar all day to avoid the missus. He was an eager apprentice when they had introduced him to the "slydial" calling app. He wondered if he could glean any other new moves while Caroline was in the back office with Brandy.

"See? You just plug this little flash drive into the port on the side of the laptop," Caroline said. She sat down at the computer and started typing through a series of screens. "Ok, it's downloading. This will take a couple minutes. Once it's done, we can run the program and see if it catches anything unusual."

Caroline's back was to the bar, but she could hear Danny's voice.

"Who's he talking to?" she asked Brandy. "I don't want to turn around and have him think I'm looking. Is it some girl?"

"No. He's sitting between two retired old men."

"Oh," Caroline said as she laughed at herself.

"What did Danny ever do to you that you think you have to keep him on such a tight leash?"

"He didn't do anything. It's men in general. And he's a man. So, you always have to be on your guard. You never know when they're going to give into their savage ways."

"Seems like all this stalking and tracking is harder on you than it is on him."

Caroline just shrugged. "Small price to pay."

She glanced over at the computer. "Ok, it's done downloading. Now we let it work its magic." She again keyed in some information and soon a swirly icon was circling on the computer screen to indicate something was happening. After a couple of minutes, a report popped up on the screen. Caroline clicked to enlarge it.

"Ok. Are you ready?" she said excitedly.

"I don't know," Brandy said. "I'm kind of nervous. What if he actually did it?"

"That's what you want, right? You want to catch the guy and bring him down!"

"Yeah, but it's so weird to think it's someone I know. That he could have been hiding in plain sight this whole time. All the investigation has been fun, but now that there might be a face to it, it just freaks me out a little bit."

"Alright, what do we have here," Caroline said scanning the report. "This breaks down the keystrokes by date and then further breaks them down by time so you can distinguish exactly who was on the computer. I just ran it back to the beginning of the month. Here, why don't you sit down and look through it. You'll know better than I will what looks like normal activity and what doesn't."

Caroline switched chairs with Brandy. Now, Brandy's back was to the bar and Caroline could see out the office door. "Wonder what's so funny?" Caroline said as she watched Danny laugh with Big Joe and Ralph.

"Let him have his fun, Caroline. They aren't talking about you, if that's what you're worried about."

Caroline continued to watch Danny like a hawk as Brandy surveyed the software's search results.

Brandy abruptly started laughing, temporarily causing Caroline to break her stare.

"What?" Caroline said, as Brandy guffawed so hard she could barely speak.

"Look at this!" she pointed to a log of keystrokes on the first day of the month at approximately 11:00 a.m.

Caroline read out loud. "Megan Markle wedding photos; Royal Wedding fascinators. Yeah, so what?" she asked.

"Keep going," Brandy said, still laughing and wiping mascara away from her eyes as it streamed down her cheeks.

"Beyoncé's twins; Beyoncé hair flip; Beyoncé House of Dereon Fashions. What?" Caroline said, "I don't get it."

"That was Chaz. Chaz searched for those things. Oh my gosh, this is cracking me up so bad."

"Chaz the little yacht skipper who pretends to be your boss?"

"Yes, that millennial mama's boy. He comes in here acting all cool when his friends are around. He annoys the crap out of me because he'll come back behind the bar and tap beers for his friends. He just makes a mess and gets in the way. He's always trying to act like a big shot. Meanwhile, he's waiting for me to get to work and he's kicking back searching for Megan Markle's wedding photos and pictures of Beyoncé's babies." Saying it out loud caused her break down in fitful laugher again.

After a minute of unbridled giggling, Brandy finally composed herself enough to look at the rest of the report. She pointed out the details—or lack thereof—to Caroline.

"Ok. So, see right here? This is the date when the health inspector hooked his phone up to my computer. It doesn't show any keystrokes. Nothing. Does that mean he didn't type anything into the computer?"

"Yep."

"And to download anything off the computer he would have had to for sure type something, right?"

"Yes. I can't think of any way around it. You can't just plug in a phone and have it suck files from the computer without the computer being given some kind of command to cooperate. So, I hate to say it, but he's not your guy. Or, at least, he didn't download anything from your computer. Looks like he really did just use it to charge his phone."

Brandy sat and thought for a minute.

"Then I guess that means he really is interested in Ginny. He might have still taken my bank records though. I'm not ready to let him off the hook just yet. Where else could they be? That's not just a coincidence."

"What would the health inspector want with a pile of random credit card statements? Think about it," Caroline said.

"I have. I've thought it about it a lot. Maybe he's not working alone and was sent by someone else to retrieve them."

"I guess anything's possible."

"That's the whole problem," Brandy said. "Anything's possible."

*   *   *

The next day, Brandy reported to Ginny that she was still skeptical about James, but that he had not illegally downloaded anything from the office computer. Therefore, Ginny's job was to find out if he took the bank statements or, in the alternative, who at the bar had a close personal or professional relationship with him such that he might be willing to use his unfettered access to the bar to gather intelligence. Brandy could then try to figure out who among them might try to thwart her investigation.

She also gave Ginny another reminder—or warning.

"He really does like you. So, that's our ace in the hole. He'll be trying to impress you. He'll be very talkative. Use it all to your advantage."

"Brandy," Ginny said as if it were a complete sentence. "I have no idea what I'm doing. I don't know how to 'use' anything to my advantage. I don't even know what I have. I'm so nervous. Oh my gosh, I don't want to do this. Please don't make me do this. You don't have to mow my lawn."

"I already texted him the high sign. He's going to be here any minute. Just be cool. You don't have to actually go out with him tonight. He's probably just going to ask you out for a different night. And if he doesn't, then we'll figure out how you can ask him out."

"I have to ask him out??" Ginny said. "I can't ask a man out. How could I ever do that? I think I would die first. Brandyyyy," she whined.

"You've got this," Brandy said.

"Dad would be so mad that you're making me do this," Ginny said, invoking the holy spirit of their dearly departed father who was often used as a trump card in sibling battles.

"If Dad was here, the only thing he would be mad about is your pioneer dress."

Ginny started to open her mouth to respond but Brandy immediately shushed her while giving a sideways glance toward the door. "He's here," she whispered.

"I think I'm going to throw up," Ginny said. Then she leaned toward Brandy and whispered, "Do I really look like a pioneer?"

"Hi James. What brings you in on a Friday night?" Brandy said with a coy look at Ginny, who was looking peaked with worry.

"I'm done with my inspections for the week, so I thought I'd just stop in for a drink before I head home. Hi, Ginny," he said. "Do you mind if I sit here?" He politely gestured toward an empty bar stool next to her.

"Oh, yes. That's fine," Ginny said while her expression barely masked her opposite sentiments.

James sat down and clasped his hands in front of him. He looked at the call drinks on the back of the bar, but Brandy could tell he wasn't really internalizing them or making a selection. He was trying to figure out what to say.

"So, what can I set you up with, James? What's your Friday-after-work drink?"

"Oh, gosh. I don't know . . . um . . . what do you recommend, Ginny?"

"Me?" Ginny seemed surprised at being called on for an endorsement.

"Ginny just always has a Bailey's on ice."

"I don't know if I could do that one. Doesn't that have cream in it? I'm lactose intolerant."

"Oh," Brandy said as she reconsidered his options.

"I'll have a Manhattan," James said suddenly.

Brandy wasn't sure if he really wanted one or if he just thought it sounded like something "cool" to order in front of Ginny. Brandy decided to test him.

"Rye or Bourbon?"

"Rye," he said. He passed the first test. Time for test number two.

"Dry or Perfect?"

"Neither. Just a Manhattan."

"Coming right up," Brandy said with a flourish. He actually knew how to order a Manhattan. She was impressed. He seemed to sense Brandy's respect.

"I usually just order beer," he confessed. "But, I thought, 'why not have a Manhattan?'"

So, he *was* just trying to impress Ginny. Brandy made a mental note to inform Ginny of the importance of their little drink-ordering exchange later.

GINNY'S AMISH APHRODISIAC

James may know how to order a Manhattan, but Ginny may know a thing or two herself. She'll order a demure Bailey's on ice on a first meeting, but when she wants to pull out all the stops, she has a Manhattan recipe of her own:

Ingredients:

1.5 oz Maker's Mark
.75 oz Hiram Walker Crème de Banana
.75 oz Cinzano Rosso Sweet Vermouth

Preparation:

To Build Cocktail:

Stir all ingredients with ice in mixing glass for 30 seconds.
Strain into rocks glass over fresh ice.
Garnish with a fresh orange slice in the glass.

Notes:

This is riff on a perfect Manhattan using banana liqueur in lieu of dry vermouth. The ratio of sweet ingredients to whiskey is higher than a typical Manhattan.

CHAPTER EIGHTEEN

As Brandy slid James his Manhattan, the Chief walked in. Brandy cracked open a Modelo for him before he had made it to his barstool.

"Ah, thank you, darlin.'"

"My pleasure," Brandy said. She then quietly explained that the health inspector was interested in Ginny but that he might also be involved in the electronic pickpocketing. She told him that Ginny had reluctantly agreed to go on a date with James in order to gather intelligence but was now feeling nervous.

Ginny gave Papí a pleading glance, but he only gave her a wink that said, "you're fine." He had tried in vain to set her up before, but she always found excuses to thwart his efforts. So, he was glad Brandy had finally succeeded in getting her to go on a date—even if it was with an ulterior motive. And Papí would make sure she was safe. He wouldn't throw her into the clutches of a common criminal.

"I have something for you," he said to Brandy. He pulled some folded papers from the breast pocket on his uniform shirt.

"Is this the stuff from the other victims that I asked you for?"

"Yes. Well, some of it. I actually decided to analyze it for you—you know, like a real police officer."

Brandy chuckled.

"I pulled the reports and sorted through them and one in particular jumped out at me. I think it's the only one you need." He uncrumpled and smoothed the paper.

"What is it?"

"This is from a couple—a husband and wife. They called in a complaint after their credit was stolen but, get this . . . of all the complainants, they are the only ones who actually had a credit monitoring subscription to one of those services that tries to prevent identity theft. Well, it actually worked! They had gone to the gas station, to the Red Box outside the grocery store, and to pick up a pizza and by the time they got home, they were already starting to get alerts from the credit monitoring company. So, they called us to take a report."

"Did anybody follow up? How do you think that relates to my credit theft?"

"Well, it seems obvious now. Whoever is doing this, probably installed a skimmer at the gas pump or the Red Box. Those are notoriously susceptible to credit hackers because the machines are outside and accessible to the public 24/7."

"Okay. So, did you try to look at any video footage from the gas station or the store? Did you go check and see if the skimmers are still installed."

"I asked about the videos, but the grocery store doesn't keep videos for more than a week and the guy at the gas station didn't even know how to access his—you'd be surprised how often we can't get at video footage just because of inept business owners. And I did go check out the gas pump and the Red Box—the skimmers are gone, but I'm not surprised. They only install them for a day or two—anything longer and an obvious pattern emerges and becomes too easy to track. So, they move the device every couple of days. But they probably just move it to another gas pump or Red Box if the device is already retrofitted for that kind of machine. If it keeps working, they'll keep using it."

"The gas pump I can understand, but Red Box? Who even rents DVDs anymore?"

"They might not have installed the device at Red Box, I'm just speculating that it had to be the gas pump or Red Box since those are the places the couple went just before the alert was triggered by their credit monitor and because those machines can be easily manipulated with a skimmer."

"So, we have lazy cops looking for lazy criminals?" Brandy laughed with a wink.

"Heyyy," he scolded. "I resemble that remark!"

They laughed before Brandy continued.

"Did you look to find out if the people who called in complaints had cards embedded with radio technology versus an electronic strip?"

"Yes. Only a couple of them have the radio-enacted cards. The vast majority have electronic cards. I guess those radio cards are too susceptible to crowd-hacking and have mostly been replaced with the electronic cards."

"Oooh, Papí. You've been doing your homework," Brandy said, impressed by his follow-through.

"Not bad for a lazy cop," he said as he raised his Modelo in a friendly 'cheers.'

"So, that means whoever is doing this has to physically run the card through an actual device," Brandy said.

"If I understand correctly, yes."

"Thank you, Papí! We are actually getting somewhere! See? This isn't that hard. If you guys would have just scrutinized these reports in the beginning, you could have caught these guys by now."

"I don't know, Chula. We've got a long way to go. There are a lot of gas pumps in this city. And you're the one who figured out how to narrow down the field of suspects based on the type of cards that were stolen."

"But your guys could do that too and they could probably do it easier than me. My point is that these crimes are solvable. You shouldn't be so quick to give up on them because it's hard to catch a break."

"You forget, though. These aren't the only crimes we're dealing with. Someone called in a bomb threat at the high school last week. We have to drop everything. Someone robbed the credit union on Greenfield Avenue again. I can't pull a detective off that case because someone stole a credit card. We're a small department with a limited budget. I only took the time to look into this because you asked me to and because it's for *you*."

"I get it. It's just frustrating to think how all those people feel—their credit got wiped out. They worry that some psycho knows their address and social security number. They are afraid someone is selling that information to God-knows-who on the dark web. It's makes you feel exposed. It makes me feel exposed and I have a direct line to the Chief of Police. Feeling like the cops can't be bothered to investigate probably makes them hesitant to call for help."

"Your Dad would be very proud of you. I know I am."

Brandy felt bad for condemning the Chief's priorities. She wondered if she should just let it go. Why should she stress herself out by having to question everyone around her and secretly set-them up to be investigated? Her job was to help people forget. It was a cruel irony that nothing could reciprocate for her. She couldn't drop it. The sense of injustice and abject unfairness was unrelenting.

She also thought about Emily and started to feel guilty. Emily had been punishing Eric every way but Tuesday while Brandy was singularly focused on a credit theft that, in the end, really wasn't going to change her life. She considered whether she was making a bigger deal out of it than it really was so she wouldn't have to deal with the things that really did affect her: like the traumatic end of a two-year relationship.

She thought very hard about why she continued to push the investigation and why she was so bothered that the police were doing nothing helpful. She realized it really wasn't all about her. It was about Papí. She worried that the fact the police were doing nothing meant what Peter told her was true: that he had lost control of the department, that they no longer respected him, and that the community was worse off because of it. She didn't want to believe that, and by proving the crime was solvable, she was proving Papí still had value to the department and the community. She was vindicating his reputation. She would be shining a light on all the things she knew to be true about him and that nobody else seemed to give him credit for.

For Brandy the real injustice wasn't that her credit had been stolen and the police didn't give the crime high priority, it was that Papí had lost credibility and he seemed willing to rest on what others thought of him—even if it wasn't true. He wasn't advocating for himself in the same way Brandy didn't advocate for herself when Eric turned out to be a total cheater. She stuffed it down and let Emily do her dirty work. Well, if the Chief felt beaten down and couldn't advocate for himself, she would do it for him.

So, she was going to solve the case and make sure he got the credit he deserved. She felt a surge of confidence that she hadn't felt in a long time.

She looked over at Ginny sitting next to James at the bar. Ginny's expression had softened. She didn't look quite as terrified, but her pallor was still milky white. James had finished his Manhattan while Ginny had let her Bailey's melt into a sweaty mix of separated cream and water.

"You ready for another one, James?" Brandy asked.

"No, thanks. I'm good," he said as he nervously spun the empty glass.

Brandy stood with her back against the bar. She pretended to scroll through her phone but was eavesdropping on every word.

"So, Ginny. I know we don't know each other very well, but it would be really nice to get to know you better. So, um, I was wondering if, um, you would want to go um," he paused and swallowed hard. "Sometimes, at the library, I volunteer as a basic skills learning instructor. I help people learn to read and I wondered if you would want to go there and volunteer with me on Tuesday."

He braced himself for her response.

But Ginny genuinely smiled. "I volunteer at the library, too," she said. "How have I never seen you there before?"

"Which branch? I usually volunteer at the downtown branch by the courthouse."

"Ohh. Ok. I volunteer at the West Allis library."

"Well, we could go to your library," James offered.

"Oh no. I would love to go downtown. It's such an adventure. The library is so big!"

Brandy, still pretending to scroll, stifled a laugh. She would have never guessed that James would ask Ginny to volunteer at the library. *What a couple of dorks.* Brandy thought. She secretly snapped a picture of them and sent it to Peter.

"Look what I just did," she texted.

"Let me guess," Peter responded. "You hosted the bar's first-ever American Gothic look-alike contest?"

As Brandy was responding, a second text popped up on her screen.

"Is that the same woman that was following me around? It looks just like her! Is she stalking you now too?"

Crap. Brandy forgot that Peter had already seen Ginny—though, unwittingly.

"Um . . . that's my little sister," Brandy admitted. "And I may have just set her up with her perfect match."

"Good on you, because if she's the same person who was trying to talk to me at the gym and was following me at the grocery store, she needs all the help she can get!"

Again, before Brandy could respond another message appeared.

"Wait. You didn't send your little sister to spy on me, did you?" He followed it with a string of laughing emojis and punctuated it with one emoji at the end of the string in a monocle with his chin in his hands as if it were contemplating a serious question.

"New number. Who 'dis?" Brandy responded, along with a string of laughing emojis. She was busted and she knew it.

*   *   *

Unbeknownst to Brandy, across town Emily was still on a tear. She was making her last stand in punishment of Eric. Brandy had told Emily what Peter said—about how she should just give the wallet back.

Emily agreed, but only because she was worried that if she didn't and continued to harass Eric, it would look bad for Brandy. Peter still didn't know Brandy very well and Emily didn't want Peter to judge her by Emily's actions. She also didn't want it to look like Brandy wasn't over Eric and was still secretly egging Emily on. So, as much as Emily hated to retire her retribution, she agreed to give it up for the greater good.

But not without one final turning of the screws.

Emily texted Eric one final time and after calling him some creative insults, she told him she would part with his wallet on the condition he never contact Brandy again and let her live in peace. If he would abide by those terms, Emily would let him live in peace, as well.

He responded with a text that called her a name that any self-respecting female dog would find unflattering.

"You must not want your wallet very bad. Never mind," she said.

He back-pedaled and said he really did want it.

She told him he could find it in his yard.

After about an hour of searching and several unanswered texts asking for clues as to where it could be, Eric found a wallet. It wasn't his wallet. It was a cheap crappy Velcro wallet. Inside, it had all of Eric's belongings organized. His credit cards and pre-paid VISAs were all neatly installed in the interior slots. Cash was in the top fold. This wallet was not vintage black leather but was lime green nylon decorated with soccer balls. Inside was a handwritten note.

"So, you'll never forget who has you by the balls."

CHAPTER NINETEEN

Brandy and Peter sat across from each other under a broad umbrella on the cobblestone patio of Café Hollander. Hairy dutifully laid at Brandy's feet with a collapsible water bowl filled to the brim. Brandy and Peter were on another lunch date and, as usual, drew the scrutiny of onlookers. Peter swore it was because Brandy is so pretty, but the truth became evident as more than one diner passed by their table and thanked Peter for his service. He got a lot of attention whenever he was in uniform and it flattered Brandy almost as much as it annoyed Peter. She felt protected and a little bit famous by association. He felt conspicuous and like he was always "on duty." But it turned out they were only flattering themselves. Twice as many people who stopped to thank Peter stopped to admire Hairy, instead—asking what breed he was and if they could pet him. Hairy loved the attention.

"I think he likes you," Brandy said to Peter. "He approves."

"Approves of what?" Peter said as if he wanted to make Brandy say what he was already thinking.

"Of us," she said, giving in.

"So, we're an 'us' now?" Peter said smugly, trying not to reveal that he was really soaring inside.

"I mean, if you want to be," Brandy said. "If not, of course, I have *lots* of other options. Brownout *does* have his own ten-speed . . ."

"Well, I better snatch you up then if that's my competition. All I have to offer is a stable job with benefits, my own house, a normal family, and boring hobbies."

"Yeah, but I'm willing to overlook all that because you're so handsome."

Peter reached across the table to hold Brandy's hand. They chatted and ate and continued to entertain interruptions from Hairy's many admirers. In between, Peter teased Brandy mercilessly about sicking Ginny on him.

"I didn't have her follow you to find out if you had a girlfriend!" Brandy insisted. "I wanted to know what your routine was and where all you go so I could see if there was a pattern that matched up with anyplace I go or that Big Joe goes. I was hoping to narrow down where these crowd-hackers might lurk. The surveillance was entirely on the up-and-up and was for the greater good. I was crime-solving, not crime-seeking," she said in her defense.

"So, why didn't you just ask me, then?"

"Because we'd only known each other for, like, a week. You would think I'm some psycho stalker if I asked you to detail every place you go each week."

"And now I don't think it, I know it," he teased.

"Haha. You'll see. I'm getting close to cracking this case. But since you can't be bothered to do real investigative work like me, maybe you can do some minor surveillance for me while I fight crime."

"Ooh, ouch," he said at her passive-aggressive insult as he pretended to pull an imaginary dagger from his heart.

"Well, I don't know. Will it interfere with looking for stolen bikes and lost dogs?" he asked. "Because if it will, I don't think the department can take the hit. You'll have to do your own dirty work."

Brandy cocked her head sideways and smirked at his sarcasm.

"I also have to take a lot of donut breaks," he said. "Those are inviolate. So, if you can work around those, I'm all ears."

"I need you to tell me if James Fraley has any kind of criminal history I should worry about. I looked him up on the statewide circuit court database, but his name is more common than I thought. It came back with some hits, but I don't know if they are him or not. So, can you find out for me?"

He stared at her as if he were having to think really hard. She dramatically batted her eyelashes and clasped her hands together by her heart.

"Ok," he said feigning defeat.

"If you can look up the actual tickets and tell me the birthdates of the offenders, I can easily narrow it down," she said.

"If all the guy has are some traffic tickets, why bother? I hope that wouldn't scare Ginny off."

"Because they aren't just traffic tickets. The main one I'm concerned about is a ticket for disorderly conduct. I know that is a blanket charge that can cover all manner of ills."

"Oooh. Interesting. Alright. I'll check him out."

*   *   *

Later that night, Brandy and Emily decided to implement the next phase of Brandy's investigation. Brandy had already determined that the Red Box was likely not the source of the fraud because she hadn't used a Red Box. She figured it had to be the gas station—especially if the station owner was asleep at the wheel or seemed as incompetent at managing his security as the Chief described.

Brandy wanted to check out the scene for herself and see if, by chance, any skimmers had been reinstalled at the gas station. She also wanted to get a feel for how easy or hard it would be to install a skimmer undetected.

Emily drove. They pulled up to a pump outside the small convenience store and car wash.

"I really don't need gas," Emily said. "What should I do?"

"Get some anyway."

"But then what? We can't just sit here at the pump. Don't you have to check each and every pump's card reader?"

Brandy realized she hadn't really thought through her strategy in detail. She wanted to go check out the gas station, but she hadn't considered, as a practical matter, what that might entail. She thought for a minute.

"Alright. You get a couple bucks worth of gas and I'll check this skimmer. Then let's pull into one of the parking stalls along the side of the building. You go in and distract the cashier, so he doesn't see me tugging on all his card readers and then we'll go."

"How am I supposed to distract him? How long will it take you?"

"I don't know. Do your thing. You know, just flirt, talk, ask a lot of questions. Buy a couple of lottery tickets and take all day picking your numbers."

Emily managed to force almost four dollars' worth of gas into her car while Brandy scrutinized the card reader. It didn't look like it had been tampered with. Nothing on it was loose or broken. They pulled Emily's car to the side of the building. Once Emily was inside the store, Brandy ran from pump to pump—there were eight of them in all—jiggling parts, prying on keypads, and trying to figure out how hard it would be to tamper with the machines.

Meanwhile, inside, Emily was ready to work her magic but was inadvertently spared by a young mother who was occupying the cashier at the window. Emily stood in line with some Red Bull, pork rinds, moon pies, gum, a Slim Jim the length of her arm, several bags of hot peanuts, a bag of mini Snickers and a full-sized Whatchamacallit. She periodically glanced outside to see how far along Brandy was in her mission.

From behind, the young mother's hair was a stringy mess. She also had two toddlers with her, and one appeared to still be in diapers based on the tell-tale bulge that caused it to waddle and squish when it walked. The other child appeared to be about three years old. Both of them incessantly tried to get the woman's attention.

"Mom, mom, mom, mommyyyy," they nagged in turn. But the woman was fixated on pointing out which carton of cigarettes she wanted from a locked display behind the counter.

As the woman moved aside slightly to point to the back shelf, Emily could see she had placed a pregnancy test on the counter to be purchased along with her cancer sticks. Emily became indignant about how many kids the woman was already ignoring and how she could manage to get knocked up with another one. But she became downright judgey about the woman ordering a carton of cigarettes when she might be pregnant.

Emily couldn't help herself. "You know, second-hand smoke is harmful to babies."

The woman simultaneously swatted the three-year-old's hand away from her and turned around to stare daggers at Emily. "You should mind your own business."

Emily was stunned. Not because the woman had swatted the hand of a toddler and not because she had dared talk-back to Emily, but because Emily recognized her. It was Eric's garden-variety skank!

Brandy was still outside staking-out the pumps. She had no idea what was unfolding inside the store. Brandy was busy tugging on card readers and putting notes in her phone: "It's too well-lit and though the pumps are exposed 24/7, the gas station is actually open 24/7 as well-meaning someone is always there to catch the culprit. Too risky," she wrote.

Inside, as the woman paid for her pregnancy test and cigarettes, she hoisted the baby on her hip and yanked the toddler behind her, stopping only long enough to get a word in edge-wise while Emily paid for her loot.

The discussion turned into a loud confrontation as Emily berated her for getting knocked up by a loser who was still trying to get back together with Brandy. The woman protested, calling Emily "jealous" and insisting Eric loved her and nobody else.

Brandy overheard them exchanging words and looked up. She immediately recognized the girl too. Brandy walked over and joined the conversation, clarifying that she—and not Emily—was Eric's ex-girlfriend, nobody was "jealous," and the Skank could keep him.

"But I'm warning you," Brandy said. "He's going to do the same thing to you that he did to me. I don't know what makes you think you're so damn special that he won't. He's been trying to get back together with me since the day I left."

The girl was offended and tried to suggest she was somehow superior to Brandy and that her superiority would protect her from Eric's roving eyes.

"I'll tell you what," Brandy said. "If you're so sure of yourself, come to 'Olive or Twist' tomorrow at 1 p.m. You can catch him red-handed, I guarantee it."

"I'll be there. You're on. There ain't no way he'd do me dirty like that!" the woman said.

CHAPTER TWENTY

The next day, while Brandy was opening the bar, Ginny was on her date and fact-finding mission with James. They had decided to volunteer over the lunch hour, to make it less date-y, Ginny said. But, lunch-hour volunteering seemed like a very "Ginny" thing to do.

Peter had funneled Brandy his findings—or lack thereof—regarding James. None of the James Fraleys in the state database were him—they were all excluded based on either age or location. Brandy was relieved he did not have a disorderly conduct charge but was a little disappointed he was so squeaky clean. *What a bore!* she thought.

As Brandy went about her opening tasks, she noticed some papers shoved under the cash register and, for a second, berated herself for leaving the beer order under there again. If the beer distributor was there and she got distracted as they were running through her list, she would often shove it under the cash register. She didn't want to set it on the bar where her customers might see the wholesale prices of the beer. They would raise hell if they knew the mark-up that Chaz was getting away with.

She yanked the pages out from under the register and some of them fluttered onto the floor. As she bent to pick them up, she was simultaneously horrified and relieved. They were the bank statements she had been looking for!

She must have been looking at them and absent-mindedly shoved them under the register when she got distracted. She forgot it about it and wholly thought she had left them on the corner of the desk—so when they turned up "missing," she was sure somebody had taken them. Turns out, that "somebody" was her.

She laughed at herself, but worried Ginny wouldn't think it was so funny. Still, Brandy wanted to give Ginny an out. She texted her only two words: "my bad."

"What?" Ginny texted back, almost immediately.

"You know those bank statements I thought James stole? I found them under the cash register . . . where I left them."

"Are you kidding me??" Brandy could almost hear Ginny's tone of voice screeching through the text message.

"So, he's clean. You don't have to embarrass yourself by asking him any questions. Mission complete."

Ginny left her hanging. Brandy wasn't surprised. She knew Ginny was probably fuming. Here she was stuck on a terrifying first date with a short-sleeved health inspector who likes to teach people to read. On second thought, that sounded like Ginny's idea of a perfect date.

As her customers came in, Brandy regaled them with the legend of the missing bank statements and how they were under the cash register all along. One by one as they sat at the bar, she would play "guess what I found" before shocking them with the big reveal.

She texted both Peter and the Chief and admitted her mistake and exonerated the put-upon health inspector.

Peter responded with some jokes at Brandy's expense. The Chief responded to say that James was still on his radar if he was trying to date Ginny and he would reserve judgment until he had proven himself worthy of Ginny's attention.

In between text messages, Emily arrived at the bar. She took a seat next to Brownout which, from the size of his grin, must have flattered him greatly. She said only two words to him: "You buying?"

"Yes'm," he said. "Set my lady up with anything she wants." Emily could get any man to buy her a drink—even Brownout. But she was the worst drink orderer in town—every bartender's nightmare. She always wanted to try "craft cocktails" that she had seen on Pinterest. She had no idea what they were called or what was in them.

She tried to give Brandy some guidance. "I think it was peach-flavored but also blue."

Brandy would usually try to appease her—and as long as the end result was colorful and fruity, Emily was satisfied. When she was too busy to play mixologist, Brandy would just hand her a Tito's and soda with a lemon and a lime.

"Did you initiate mission Happy Family?" Emily asked Brandy.

"Oh, but of course," Brandy said in a sly tone. "But get a load of this. When I asked him to come here, he said, 'Ok, but don't tell Emily.'"

The girls howled in laughter at the thought of Eric running scared from the specter of Emily.

"Speak English," Brownout said. "What are you girls talking about?"

"You'll see," Brandy said.

"Oh, will you ever!" Emily exclaimed.

Brownout tried in vain to get them to reveal spoilers, but they kept telling him it would be far more entertaining if he didn't know what was coming. Soon, Ralph and Big Joe were also in on the news and they were all speculating as to what could be going on.

At high 1:00 p.m., Eric's skank arrived. Brandy asked her to sit in the office and wait.

"Because Eric is coming here any minute to try to win me back. I want you to hear it with your own ears—and not because I care about you at all, but because if you're having his baby, you need to start making decisions based on the truth—not on what you hope is true."

The girl waited in the office and soon, Eric arrived. The tension in the air was thick with awkward avoidance as he tried to pretend Emily wasn't sitting right there.

"Come here, where no one can hear us," Brandy said. "She showed him half-way down the hallway in between the bar and the office. His back was to the office so he could not see into it.

"I wanted you to come here because I've been thinking . . ." Brandy started. But before she could say more, Eric started pouring his heart out.

"She doesn't mean anything to me. I'm disgusted that I was even with her. I don't know why I did it, I swear it was only that one time. I haven't seen her since. I've only been thinking about you and trying to figure out how to win you back."

Brandy stood looking at him. Her back was to the bar and even she could feel Emily's icy glare.

"What's she doing here?" he whispered to Brandy glancing toward Emily.

"I think the bigger question is what's *she* doing here?" Brandy said as she spun him around to face his Skank.

"Angela, I didn't mean it," he started to say, but he was met with a hard slap in the face. Angela pushed past him yelling at him the whole time.

"You think you can do this to me? Well, you're stuck with me. I'm not going anywhere." Brandy wasn't sure if she was trying to assert herself to Eric or to Brandy.

"Trust me, I don't want him," Brandy said.

"Well, I don't either, but now I've got him," Angela said. "Because me and you are having a baby."

"What?!" Eric shrieked.

"And if you're going to take care of one kid, you're going to take care of all my kids. Let's see how many sluts out there want to mess with a guy with three kids under the age of three. That sounds like a good time, doesn't it? Well, welcome to your life!"

"Is this true or did you just set her up to say this?" Eric asked Brandy.

"Hey, she doesn't have anything to do with this," Ralph said, coming to Brandy's defense.

"This can't be happening. Brandy, come on. Help me," Eric pleaded.

"Help you?" Brandy laughed at the suggestion. "You made your bed. Go lie in it, you dirtbag."

"Good thing I gave you those gift cards back. Looks like you're going to need them for diapers. Hey!" Emily said, turning to Angela as if she were telling her a secret. "He's got $400 in prepaid VISA cards in his wallet right now."

Angela continued to yell and make a scene. Eric continued to beg Brandy and defend himself from Angela. Hairy started growling at Eric and that was Big Joe's cue to move the party outside. He grabbed Eric by the shirt collar and forcefully escorted him out of the bar, on dragging tiptoes.

Emily thought fast and snapped some pictures of the ruckus.

"For Facebook," she said to Brandy with a wink.

"Oh wait!" Brandy yelled. "You almost forgot these." She turned around and raced to the storage room and returned with a big obnoxious bouquet of balloons that said "Congratulations" and were decorated with pacifiers and storks.

Emily busted out laughing as she high-fived Brandy for her ingenuity.

She handed them off to Big Joe who spiked the balloons in turn at Eric before Angela yanked at the bouquet like it was a three-year-old and headed toward her car.

Back inside, they all decompressed and laughed as they took turns reenacting parts of the blow-up.

"He's lucky I didn't get up," Brownout said as he took a slow sip of his vodka.

*   *   *

Virgie and Finn arrived a little before 7 p.m. for the evening shift. Brandy had an eventful day, so she decided to reward herself with a pizza. As she transitioned the bar over to Virgie's able hands, Brandy told her all the gory details of the showdown with Eric and how life as he knew it was now over.

Virgie wasn't surprised but, as usual, had a cautionary tale to share.

"He better *hope* she's pregnant!" Virgie said.

"What do you mean? I'm sure he's praying to all that's holy it was a false alarm. The last thing he wants is a kid to take care of—let alone two more babies that aren't even his."

"That we know of," Emily said dryly.

"Yeah, that we know of," Brandy agreed.

"She might be one of those kooks who pretends to be pregnant in order to trap a man," Virgie warned. "She'll have a baby shower and everything and make a big ta'do about the whole thing. She'll stuff her shirt to fake a belly and then she'll go find some poor unsuspecting young mother in the grocery store parking lot. Next thing ya know, she cut the baby out of her belly and left her to die in the woods!"

"Virgie!" Brandy exclaimed with a discreet glance toward Finn as if to remind her she had a PG audience.

"Oh, he's fine," Virgie said. "He knows all about those things. Because I told him, if a girl ever tells you she's pregnant, you make her pee on a stick right in front of you—don't blink your eyes. Otherwise, you could end up raising a stolen baby!"

"You told him that?" Even Emily, who had zero understanding of how to raise children, was aghast. "He's eleven. And you're already preaching to him about how not to knock-up some girl?"

"You gotta start early. They teach that in school, the family lifestyles or," she paused and yelled to the end of the bar. "Finn, what's that class they make you take at school where you learn about puberty? The real name of it?"

"I don't know," he said, fixated on his tablet.

"We call it 'boner class' at home, but he don't wanna say that in front of you. Goll darn. I can't for the life of me remember what it's called. Anyway, he knows plenty."

Emily gave Brandy a wide-eyed expression and pretended to gulp down her drink as if she needed to forget the whole conversation.

Soon, the delivery man from "Pizza D'Action" arrived. Brandy, once again, hailed him as her savior and jokingly told Finn he was in charge of the bar while she ran to the back office to find her purse.

While he was waiting, Pizza Guy took note of Finn playing on his tablet.

"You still spending your grandma's hard-earned money?"

"No, I wasn't even spending it before."

"I heard somebody say you're pretty good with electronics. Do you have a gaming computer?"

"No way! Those cost, like, thousands of dollars. I just have this tablet. It used to be my mom's, but she got a new one."

"I like electronics. I'm kind of a techie. My dream is to start a tech company and be like Steve Jobs. Do you know who that is?"

"Everybody knows who Steve Jobs is," Finn said.

"He started out in his garage, so I don't feel so bad. I'm actually working on an invention right now. Do you want to see it?"

"You have it with you?"

"Yeah," the man pulled a small cell-phone sized piece of equipment from his pocket. It looked a little unsophisticated—almost like a bulky calculator.

"What is it?"

"Well, you might really like it because it solves the problem of having to use an adult's credit card and always getting in trouble when they forget they said you could buy a game."

"How does it work?" Finn asked leaning intently over the device.

"You just punch this button, and then see that little swirly icon? That means it's loading. Then once it's loaded, you hit this button and it transfers all the information."

"But what does it do?"

"It's kind of hard to explain because it's new technology. Right now, it just gathers data. But maybe you could help me test it? I need a bunch of testers before I can take it to the next level. I'd be willing to give you twenty dollars if you would just use it for a week. Wherever you go, school, church, here at the bar, just turn it on, hit the download button and then at the end of the week, I can go through the data."

"How do I for sure know you'll give me the twenty dollars?"

"Because I'm a man of my word. But you know what—just to prove it, I'll give you the twenty dollars up front. But you have to promise to keep the device top secret. You can't tell your grandma or show it to your friends or anything. If anyone finds out about it, they could steal my idea before I get a patent and I can't risk someone with more money or know-how coming along and stealing my thunder."

"Let's see the twenty dollars."

Pizza Guy pulled his wallet out of his back pocket and produced a wrinkled twenty-dollar bill.

"Ok," Finn said taking it. "I'll help you."

"Alright, buddy! We're partners. Don't forget it. When one of us becomes Steve Jobs we can't forget the other one, ok?"

"Ok."

"I'll be back next week sometime. Until then, remember, download every day and keep it secret. We might even be able to get a deal on *Shark Tank*!"

Virgie had been holding court under the TV and arguing with Brownout about whether or not Judge Judy was a real judge. She was oblivious to Finn's conversation. Brandy finally came around the corner of the bar.

"Hey, sorry it took me so long. I got stopped by one of the upstairs tenants. How much is it? Eleven dollars?"

"Yeah," Pizza Guy said with a wink at Finn.

Brandy paid him and he left through the side door. Brandy was starving but offered Finn a piece of pizza first. He gladly accepted as he quietly tucked the twenty dollars and the device into his backpack along with his tablet.

CHAPTER TWENTY-ONE

"Soooo?" Brandy said as soon as Ginny answered the phone.
"So, what?" Ginny asked as if she had no idea.

"How was the date with James? Did you go through with it after I told you that you could beg off? Fill me in?"

"Of course, I went through with it."

The phone was silent.

"And what about it? I mean, did you have fun? Did you like him? Did it turn into a 'real date?' You can't just leave me hanging."

"Why are you so interested in my personal life all of a sudden?" She was stalling and trying to change the subject.

"What makes you think you *have* a personal life all of a sudden? All you do is hang out with me and babysit my dog. So, if you suddenly have a personal life, you need to spill it. After all, I told you everything about Eric. Everything."

"Yeah, but I didn't ask for that."

"You never told me not to tell you. Besides, that story was pure entertainment. That was probably better than one of your little mystery books. I bet you didn't have to read for a week because of all the fodder I gave you from *my* personal life."

"Your real-life problems are no substitution for my books. Don't flatter yourself."

"Ok, we've small-talked enough. Do you like him or not?"

"Yes."

"Ok. Now, we're getting somewhere!"

The phone was again silent.

"Ginnyyy," Brandy sang. "You like him! That's exciting. So, what's next? Are you going to go out with him again?"

"Yes, but only to discuss business."

"Business? Is that what you call it?" Brandy said in a snide tone before singing "*Bow chicka bow bow.*"

"We decided to partner up on a little project."

"For real?" Brandy was surprised. "What kind of project?"

"We're going to write a book together."

Brandy started laughing. "Are you serious? What do you know about writing books?"

"Plenty. I read all the time. It can't be that hard. Besides, James is a published author."

"Published author?" Brandy was indignant. "What has he published? A 'How To' book on the proper washing and storing or garnishes?"

"He's actually a published mystery writer. And he wants me to help him write his next mystery."

"Wait, real mysteries or the kind with cupcakes and cats like you read?"

"My cozy books are real mysteries. And that's actually the kind he writes if you must know. He uses a pen name. And I think we will be a great team. I have a lot of ideas. Every time I read a cozy, I think about funny things the characters could do or about better ways to investigate the crime. I told him some of my ideas and he loved them."

"He's probably just saying that because he wants to get in your frock or muumuu or whatever it is you call it."

"He's not like that at all."

"All men are like that."

"Not James."

"You'll learn. Ok. So, tell me these great ideas that he loved so much."

"Ok. Are you ready?" Ginny said, trying to heighten the suspense. "We are writing about . . . a witch cop."

"That's dumb. Nobody would read that."

"Yes, they would! You don't know because you only read the super popular mainstream books."

"They're called 'classics.'"

"They're called 'boring.' There's a whole genre of cozy books about witches who solve crime. Ours is going to put a different spin on it, of course."

"Let me know when you've jumped ahead of Stephen King in the rankings. Until then, God speed."

"You'll see. This is why I didn't want to even tell you about it. Because I knew you would just make fun of it."

"I'm sorry. I'll try to be nice. I'm happy if you like James. And if you guys have things in common that you can to do together all the better."

Before Ginny could answer, Brandy screamed into the phone as if she had been injured.

"Brandy? Hello?" The other end of the phone was silent. "What happened?"

"I can't believe this! Are you kidding me?"

"What?" Ginny demanded with concern in her voice.

"I was standing here opening the mail while we talked. I just tore into some kind of bill and it shows a three-thousand-dollar charge at a Hyundai dealership!"

"Are you sure it's your mail? Look at the name again."

"Yes, it's my mail. It says right on it, 'Brandy Alexander.' It has my address and everything. It's from some credit card company I don't even recognize. I thought it was just some stupid credit card offer and it's a bill! I knew this was going to happen! I knew as soon as my credit was stolen that it was only a matter of time until some loser sold it on the dark web. Now anybody can just open credit cards in my name. This is unbelievable! I am so mad!"

She was yelling into the phone. Ginny couldn't get Brandy's attention.

"I've gotta go," Brandy said unapologetically. She hung up the phone and immediately looked up the number of the Hyundai dealership listed on the statement.

"Hello, can I speak to your billing or accounting department?"

She angrily suffered through a series of energetic Hyundai ads while she was on hold. Finally, a human who introduced herself as "Karen" answered.

"Yes, my name's Brandy Alexander and I just received a credit card statement showing a three-thousand-dollar charge at your business and I've never been there in my life. I don't own a Hyundai. Can you please look into this and let me know if there has been some kind of mistake?"

As Karen took down information regarding the date of the transaction and amount, Brandy complained that her credit had been stolen and she was afraid this charge was on an account that had been fraudulently opened.

"Can I just bring this statement down to your office? I would like to talk directly to whoever is in charge. I'm not saying it's your fault, but I want to make sure I'm not responsible for this and I'd like to find out if you have any way of finding out who made this charge—maybe surveillance video or you can ask around and see if any of your salesmen remember."

Karen agreed to meet with Brandy. Brandy turned around and called Emily to accompany her. Brandy was livid and frustrated and needed some moral support. Emily would also make sure Brandy didn't say anything she'd regret and, if she did, at least Emily would be there as a witness to Brandy's side of the story.

While Brandy waited for Emily to pick her up, she called the credit card company and about lost her mind when they refused to give her any information because she did not know the password or PIN number to the account.

"But that's the whole problem. I didn't set up the account. That's why I'm calling you. Somebody else set this up fraudulently and I'm trying to shut it down."

She breathed heavy as she tried to listen to the customer service representative on the other end of the phone.

"So, basically, what you're telling me is that if someone steals my identity and uses it to fraudulently set up an account by creating passwords and PINs I obviously don't know about—then only the thief can have access to the account? This is insane!"

The customer service representative tried to explain that they could not just close accounts because somebody called and claimed fraud—Brandy could be a disgruntled ex-wife or vindictive employee or anybody. Without confirmation from Brandy or the cardholder, they could do nothing.

"But my name is on the card—you have my address. You are sending ME the bill."

The service rep suggested he could be more helpful if Brandy had purchased credit protection.

"Why would I purchase credit protection for a card I didn't even know I had and that somebody else opened by stealing my identity?" Brandy wished she was on an old-fashioned rotary phone so she could slam the receiver down with flair. But, instead, she just furiously tapped the "end call" button as she ran out the door to meet Emily.

On the way to the car dealership, Matt called Brandy. She forgot to leave a check for the beer distributor so he asked if she could swing by. The beer distributor was waiting. They didn't work on credit because Chaz was a young and untested bar-owner. He hadn't built enough of a relationship with his suppliers to gain their trust. Brandy had, but she wasn't the boss, so she was bound to give the beer guy a check—her word was good, but not good enough. Brandy was able to sign checks—but it was Chaz's money that backed them up. She wished he would lift a finger once in a while to build the relationships that would make the bar run smoother.

Emily waited in the car while Brandy ran inside "Olive or Twist." Brandy went into the office to write the check and when she opened the desk drawer, found a little surprise.

"Matt, is this your phone?" she yelled out to the bar.

Matt poked his head into the office and looked at the heavy black contraption she was holding up for his inspection.

"Nope. That's not mine."

"Whose is it? Did somebody forget it at the bar? Has anybody called for it?"

"No. Actually, your friend dropped that off. What's his name? The one with the bossy girlfriend that's always watching him like a hawk?"

"Danny?"

"Yeah, that's him. He stopped by and said he had some business to take care of and asked if he could just leave his phone here. I said 'ok' because he's your friend and he comes in once in a while."

"That's the weirdest thing I've ever heard," Brandy said. "Why would he need to leave his phone here of all places?"

"I don't know. I didn't think it was a big deal. I just put it in the drawer so nothing would happen to it."

"Something's up. And I do NOT want to be in the middle of it," Brandy said under her breath as she wrote out the check.

Back in the car with Emily, she couldn't help but share what Matt had just told her.

"Why would he need to leave his phone at the bar?" Emily wondered aloud.

"I know, right? So weird. And so awkward. It has to have something to do with Caroline and how she tracks him constantly. I'm sure he wanted to go somewhere without her knowing, but where and why?"

"I hope it's nothing bad. Do we say anything to Caroline? What do we do?"

"I don't know. I mean, he didn't even leave his phone behind when he went to buy her engagement ring. She tracked him right to the store. So, where could he possibly be going that he doesn't want her to know about?"

"He wouldn't cheat on her," Emily said. "No way. He doesn't have it in him. And he knows better. Caroline would find out. No way."

"But what else would he be doing? He's not going to try to conceal his location just to go do something totally benign."

"True," Emily said.

They agreed to leave that lead open-ended for now. They had bigger issues to deal with at the moment.

They walked into the Hyundai dealership and, as usual when Emily and Brandy went anywhere together, all the men's heads turned. There was a fairly obvious race to see who could "be of assistance" first.

Brandy approached the welcome desk and said she was there to meet with Karen. They were offered a seat in the waiting room which doubled as a waiting area for the service department. There, they could watch daytime television and make their own cappuccinos in paper cups. They ably deflected a few more eager salesmen who offered assistance before Karen finally greeted them.

She walked them to a cubicle surrounded by high glass walls. It was open at the front and offered little privacy. Emily and Brandy seated themselves opposite Karen who sat at a computer.

"I did a little looking," Karen said. "Apparently, it was your husband that purchased a vehicle."

CHAPTER TWENTY-TWO

"My husband?" Brandy shrieked. Emily immediately put a hand on Brandy's thigh as a subtle message to keep control of herself.

"Yes, you should have received the spousal notification in the mail."

"First of all, I don't have a husband. Second of all, I received no such notice."

Karen looked stricken.

"Are you divorced? Or separated?"

"No," Brandy yelled. "I've never been married in my life. I don't have a husband. So, you better explain to me right now how 'my husband' bought a car from you."

"Um, hang on one minute please," Karen said, putting a finger up. She picked up the desk phone and dialed a number. She spoke discreetly to whoever answered.

Almost as soon as she hung up a man interrupted them. He poked his head around the corner while gripping the glass wall with both hands.

"Mrs. Dixon?" he asked.

Brandy stood up and simultaneously almost jumped out of her skin.

"Mrs. Dixon? What is going on? My last name is 'Alexander.' And I'm not married. Somebody, please tell me what is going on."

"Ma'am, please. Keep your voice down. We'll get this figured out. Can you ladies come with me, please?"

"Who are you?"

"I'm Thomas, I'm the sales manager. Let's go back to my office."

Brandy angrily tossed her purse over her shoulder. Emily followed. As soon as they got into Thomas's office, Brandy unloaded.

"I'm kind of freaking out here because you just called me Mrs. Dixon and that's not my name and I'm not married, but you think I'm married but Dixon is my boyfriend's last name. Well, he's kind of my boyfriend, but anyway, he's a cop and I just . . . what is going on? What is happening?"

Thomas spoke in a calm voice. He tried his best to be accommodating—reassuring them he was going to help; that he would get to the bottom of things; that he needed Brandy to calm down and answer some questions.

"Sit down, Brandy," Emily encouraged. "Just, settle down. Listen to what he has to say. He's trying to help you."

Brandy was nearly shaking with fury and fear. She had no idea what to expect.

"I'm Thomas Miller. I'm in charge of the salesmen. First, I just want to say, I believe you. I believe you had nothing to do with the transaction. But I need you to help us figure out who this is that claimed to be your husband."

"Ok," Brandy said, trying to calm down.

Thomas first asked to see Brandy's I.D. Normally, Brandy would have been insulted, but she was glad he was now being cautious. She wondered if they checked the I.D. of her "husband" before he drove off in that new Hyundai. Thomas wrote down Brandy's full name and address, handed her I.D. back to her and started typing on his computer.

"Ok. Let's see," he said squinting at his computer screen. "And may I see the credit card statement with the charge?"

She eagerly handed it over. He continued to tap away at his keyboard.

"Based on the details in your credit card statement, I can tie that transaction to a sale that Diana handled. She's one of our newer sales girls. I'm going to page her to see if she can come over here."

He picked up the desk phone which also apparently served as some kind of intercom and made an announcement for Diana Metz to come to his office. He then continued to stare at his computer screen as he murmured about what he was seeing.

"I pulled up the invoice. Looks like we sold a brand-new Hyundai Tucson on the date in question—actually, I take that back. We ordered it—it was a custom vehicle. When we do that, we have the customer pay their down payment, but we don't actually charge the card or cash the check until the vehicle is shipped to us. So, looks like he ordered it and then, whenever it was shipped was when your card was charged."

"But, who did it?" Brandy asked.

"Let's see, customer name: Peter Dixon."

Brandy's eyes started to fill with tears. "Emily," she said. She could say no more.

"It's ok. It's probably a mistake. He wouldn't do that to you. It's ok," Emily said.

Thomas, clearly feeling very awkward about the whole situation said, "I take it you know him?"

Brandy shook her head yes. "First Eric and now this," she said quietly to Emily.

"It's not right. It can't be," Emily said. "It's ok. It's ok." She was willing it to be so, but even Emily was shaken.

"And I take it he's not your husband?" Thomas said.

"No. He's my boyfriend. Or, he was. I guess," Brandy wanted to sob but she tried to maintain her composure and didn't want to succumb to defeat. She had already been cheated on and taken advantage of. She couldn't bear to admit to herself that she let it happen again.

Diana popped her head into the office. "You wanted to see me?" she asked.

"Yeah," Thomas said, motioning for her to come in.

"So, you sold a car—a custom order Tucson—to a Peter Dixon earlier this month. Apparently, he lied on his customer application and said he was married to this nice lady here. He used a credit card in her name to make his down payment and long story short, they aren't married, and she knew nothing about it."

"Ma'am," Diana said gently after reading the room, "Would you recognize him if I showed you his picture?"

"You have his picture?" Emily asked.

"I think so. Whenever somebody buys a new car, we take their picture next to it and we hang it in our 'Hall of Hyundai.' I think I remember the guy. I don't know if his picture is still up or not. Hang on."

Diana put everyone on pause and quickly left the room. Brandy's shoulders sunk.

"Hey, at least you'll know. You won't have to wonder," Emily said, holding her hand. Brandy dabbed at her eyes, careful not to let any tears actually fall. She felt sick to her stomach as she thought about how sweet Peter had been to her and how he explicitly said he wanted to take their relationship further and it was all a lie. It was almost more than she could bear.

"Here he is," Diana said as she whipped around the corner.

Emily snatched the picture from her hands. As she and Brandy fixed their eyes, they both started screaming. "What?! Oh my God!! No!"

It wasn't Peter Dixon at all.

*   *   *

Back at "Olive or Twist," James was waiting for Ginny. They had agreed to hold their first "business meeting" there. They both pretended it was a meeting out of sheer convenience—to talk about the book. But it was definitely a date.

Ginny was happy to meet at the bar because she knew Matt was working today. If Brandy were there, she wouldn't be able to resist teasing Ginny and making it super uncomfortable for her. Also, Matt would make her a Bloody Mary. Brandy refused to make them for Ginny after noon because Brandy claims they made Ginny "crabby" because they threw off her early-to-bed sleep cycle. Ginny thought Brandy was just making excuses because Bloody Marys are labor intensive—Brandy was a purist and refused to use a Bloody Mary mix like every other cheap bar in town. She insisted on making them from scratch—except when Ginny wanted one.

When Ginny arrived, James gallantly stood to greet her and made an awkward attempt to pull out her bar stool for her, but he underestimated its weight and it didn't budge with the first pull. Then, it reluctantly stuttered across the floor on the second pull.

"You don't have to do that," Ginny said. "I'm fine."

They exchanged pleasantries and Matt, having been fully and secretly informed by Brandy about James and Ginny's "relationship," treated them with the utmost discretion.

James, again, ordered a Manhattan and impressed Matt with his Manhattan know-how. Matt apparently impressed James, too, when he garnished the drink with a skewer of three Luxardo cherries.

"Are these actual Luxardo brand?" James asked, subtly showing-off his insider knowledge.

"Yep. Nothing but the best here at 'Olive or Twist,'" Matt deadpanned. "Actually, Chaz got rid of the maraschino cherries and replaced them with Luxardo cherries because he read about them in GQ and thought they were cool."

"Ha," James said. "That sounds like Chaz."

Matt then turned his attention to building Ginny's Bloody Mary. He pulled out all the stops—garnishing it with a Usinger's sausage stick, smoked mozzarella string cheese, a dill pickle spear, some pickled asparagus, celery, two crisp pieces of Neuske's bacon, and a colorful skewer of alternating olives and grape tomatoes.

"Oooh! Thank you, Matt!" Ginny marveled.

"It's not much, but it's the best I could do." He wasn't being humble. Bloody Marys elsewhere in Milwaukee came topped with everything from freshly grilled scallops to an entire fried chicken. Matt's Bloody Mary was anemic my comparison—but for a dive bar, it was a respectable effort. Ginny appreciated it all the same.

As Ginny and James were admiring each other's garnishes James suddenly jumped as a pair of hands gripped both of his shoulders.

"You be good to that little girl," a voice bellowed from behind him. It was the Chief.

"Papí!" Ginny sang. Her voice went up two octaves anytime he was around.

James turned around to shake the Chief's hand. They had, of course, met in passing many times before whenever James came to inspect the bar.

"Can I buy you a drink, Chief?"

"No, no. Not while I'm on duty. They say it's a bribe. If anyone tries to give me money or buy me anything, I have to write it down and report it. It's not worth it."

"Huh," James said. "I never realized that. I guess I never assumed people would be so bold as to try to get away with something by buying the cop a drink."

"I appreciate it, but it doesn't look right. So, I must respectfully decline," he said with a slight bow.

Matt already had the Chief's Modelo cracked open and nobody dared address whether or not it "looked right" for the Chief to be drinking in a dive bar while he was on duty.

The ubiquitous Brownout raised a glass in acknowledgment of the Chief, who raised his beer bottle in return.

The regulars were chatting, and Ginny and James were getting down to "business" when Danny returned for his phone.

"Hey, Matt. Thanks for helping me out. Do you have my phone?" Danny then did a double-take. "Oh, hey, Ginny. I hardly recognized you."

"Where's Caroline?" Ginny asked, knowing very well that Danny was on a short leash.

"She's at work. But, uh, I had some things to do."

"Oooh," she said excitedly. "James, I think we have our first mystery to solve. Why would a devoted boyfriend—who is tagged, tracked, and stalked by his girlfriend day and night—need to park his phone at 'Olive or Twist' while he 'had some things to do?' What ever could those things be?" Ginny said as she pretended to think.

"The worst is so often true," James said in a very formal tone as if he were reading from a script.

"That's from 'They Do It with Mirrors,' right? Agatha Christie?"

"None other,"

"Ha! And Brandy thinks I don't know the classics." Then turning to Danny, she said, "He's right though."

"Right about what?" Danny said, looking anxiously at his watch.

"That we like to imagine the worst, but so often, it is actually true."

"I don't know what you two are getting at, but there's nothing going on. I'm on my lunch break and I wanted to eat at 'Second Hand Smoke'—you know, that barbecue place around the corner on 76th street?"

"Yeah," Ginny said. "What about it?"

"Well, Caroline banned me from going there because the last time we went there the waitress made some comment about liking Caroline's hair color and asking where she got it colored, which implied she colors her hair. So, Caroline got all insulted because her hair is naturally black, and she doesn't color it. So, now I can never go there again. But I love their cornbread and I realized, if I leave my phone here, she'll just think I stopped by here and won't know I really ate at 'Second Hand Smoke.'"

A voice spoke up at the other end of the bar. "The force is strong in you, young Jedi." It was Ralph. He raised a glass and gave Danny a nod as he took a sip.

"Hey, I learned from the best!" Danny said, giving Ralph a thumbs-up.

Matt gave Danny his phone.

"What kind of weird phone is that anyway?" Matt asked. "It weighs a ton and looks like something they'd issue in the army."

"I don't know. My work provides it. It serves the purpose, I guess. Hey, thanks again," he said. Then waving he turned to everyone and said, "I was here for a little over an hour today in case anybody asks. Ginny, make sure to tell Brandy just in case, ok?"

"Your secret's safe with me. But you do have a little sauce on the corner of your mouth."

"Ooh! Close one," he said as he wiped at it with the corner of his shirt sleeve.

CHAPTER TWENTY-THREE

Brandy and Emily were still freaking out. It was a picture of Eric.

"This isn't Peter Dixon," Brandy finally said. Tears were now escaping her eyes, but they were tears of relief and were no longer tears of agony and regret. "This is Eric Jenkins. He's my ex-boyfriend. Peter Dixon is my new boyfriend. I think Eric is trying to get back at me and now at Peter, too.

"How did he do this?" Emily asked. "How could he just lie about who he was? Didn't he have to show any I.D. or anything?"

Thomas asked Diana if Eric had taken any cars for a test-drive and Brandy immediately asked if Emily had given Eric that credit card with her name on it when she returned his wallet.

"No. I gave that back to you, remember? Besides, I thought that was a card you already knew about and it had gotten mixed up in his wallet by accident."

Brandy tried to focus for a second. Her mind was racing. "Yeah. You're right. I remember. So, what did he do? Did he actually open another card in my name? How did he do that? And why would he say he was Peter? I'm so confused."

Diana jumped in to defend herself. "He didn't test drive anything. I would only take his I.D. if he wanted to take a test drive. He acted like he had been shopping around and knew what he wanted. It didn't surprise me or anything. He wasn't buying a car off the lot. Usually, people only want to test drive the car they are buying."

"But didn't he have to fill out any paperwork or anything? How did he pay for the car? Did he finance it? How was he able to use Peter's name to do that?"

Thomas consulted his computer screen. "Sit tight for a second. I'm pulling up the actual sales contract."

Everyone waited anxiously.

"Here," he said turning his screen to face Brandy and Emily. "You take a look at this and see if any of this information is legit."

Brandy leaned close to the screen. "Ok. So, he wrote Peter's name, but used his own address? That's Eric's address but Peter's name. What an idiot. Why would he do that?"

"Maybe he's jealous that you're seeing Peter and wanted to get back at both of you?"

"But he wrote his own address down. And his own email address. Why wouldn't he just use his own name?"

Brandy scrutinized the purchase application. After a couple minutes, she looked up.

"I think I get it now. What a moron. He used Peter's name to buy the car—I have no idea why—but he used his own address because he gets free oil changes and tire rotations for the first 36 months and it says here they are going to mail him coupons every six months to be used toward the maintenance plan. So, he had to use his own address because he wants the free oil changes."

"Oh my gosh, it's just like the stupid sandwich punch card!" Emily said. "What a cheapskate!"

"How did he actually pay for the car?" Brandy asked. "I don't see that on the purchase agreement."

Thomas turned the screen back toward himself and started typing. "So, it looks like he used your credit card for the down payment and then he brought in a cashier's check for the remaining balance. So, same as paying cash."

"Excuse me one minute. I'm going to call Peter." Brandy stepped into the hallway while Emily and Diana and Thomas continued to commiserate about how Eric could have pulled off such a feat. Diana and Thomas were particularly concerned that it could happen again.

"It never occurred to me someone would buy a car in someone else's name out of spite," Diana said.

"But why Peter?" Emily wondered to herself.

Brandy stepped back into the room. "So, I talked to Peter."

"Ok," Thomas said. "Meanwhile, I think I have no choice but to call the police."

"Peter *is* the police," Brandy said.

*   *   *

Later that evening, Brandy was back at "Olive or Twist" to take the late shift. Matt was counting the cash drawer at the end of his shift and loitering while he did some minor side work. Brandy was telling anyone who would listen about how Eric was a cheater in more ways than one and had stolen her identity right out from under her. It appeared she had been victimized twice: once by Eric and once by some unknown electronic pickpocket.

When Brandy called Peter from the car dealership, he was angry and concerned but couldn't respond to the call or take the report since he was actually one of the "victims." He had sent another patrol officer to the dealership to gather evidence and information and Peter provided supplemental information and submitted to an interview back at the police station.

Brandy was anxiously awaiting an update, but Peter had warned her the wheels of justice don't move swiftly in West Allis unless a "real" crime is involved. Getting even with an ex-girlfriend by using her name to open a credit card—and even impersonating her new boyfriend on a purchase agreement—wasn't going to light any fires under the detectives.

Emily had some creative ideas of how to extract her own personal brand of street-justice, but Peter warned her off. He begged them not to get involved and to let the police handle it. He said their impatience could actually interfere with the investigation and to let things play out. Just because they weren't seeing tangible and immediate results didn't mean nothing was happening or that progress wasn't being made.

So, Brandy was actually happy she had to work a long late shift. It would keep her mind occupied and off the roller-coaster ride she'd been on throughout the day.

Just as Brandy was getting to the part of the story where Diana dramatically revealed "Peter Dixon's" picture from the "Hall of Hyundai," Virgie and Finn arrived.

"Virgie! Perfect timing! I was just getting to the good stuff about how Eric stole my credit to buy a car."

"He did what?" Virgie said with disgust. "Did you hear that, Finn? Brandy, tell Finn what happens to people who use other people's money without asking."

"Why? What did he do?"

"I didn't do anything," Finn said from the floor where he was kissing Hairy.

"Like hell, you didn't. He bought another twenty-dollar game on my credit card. I told him to undo it and to figure out how to get my card off his gaming account or whatever, but he didn't do it. So, now I'm taking his devices for a week. Can I put them in the office somewhere? If I hide them at home, he'll just go looking for them."

"Sure," Brandy said. "Finn, why don't you just change the account settings to delete the card?"

"I don't know how. I don't even know what she's talking about. I asked my mom, but she doesn't know either. So, I don't even get to use my tablet or anything for a week. And one of those devices isn't even mine."

Virgie had a handful of electronics she had confiscated for safe keeping. She handed them over to Brandy.

Brandy took inventory. "So, you have a tablet and a Nintendo Switch and, what is this?" she held up a phone-like device.

"That's an invention I'm testing. It's top secret."

"Did you make it?" Brandy asked.

"No. Someone else did. I'm not supposed to tell anyone about it. So, since it's not mine I don't think it's fair for Grandma to take it."

"Who gave you that?" Virgie demanded.

"Some guy," Finn said.

"You better not be taking things from 'some guy.' You're lucky you didn't get kidnapped and killed! Is this a guy you know? Is it someone at school? I thought that was just one of your little gaming consoles. He could have been some nut that set up that thing to explode in your backpack. Who gave it to you?"

"The pizza guy that brings pizza here."

"Why did he give it to you?" Brandy hoped her line of questioning would be more productive than Virgie's gloom-and-doom hyperventilating.

"He heard that I like electronics and so when he was dropping off your pizza, he said he had an invention he was working on and he asked if I would test it. He said he'd give me twenty-dollars to test it for him. But he doesn't want anyone to know because they might steal his ideas."

Brandy and Virgie exchanged horrified looks.

"So, let me get this straight. The pizza delivery guy wants an eleven-year-old kid to test his top-secret invention? Finn, does that sound right to you?"

"I don't know. What's wrong with it?"

"Normally, adults don't ask children for help. Especially with top-secret professional projects."

Virgie and Brownout were engaged in a spirited conversation—trying to one-up each other with all the nefarious things Pizza Guy's invention could do and all the tragedies it could have imposed on poor Finn.

Meanwhile, Brandy was trying to unravel this most unusual business arrangement.

"Have you tested it yet? What does the invention do?"

Finn told Brandy the whole story of how the deal was struck and what his end of the bargain entailed. He emphasized that he was sworn to secrecy and begged Brandy not to say anything for fear of someone ripping-off Pizza Guy's million-dollar idea.

Brandy felt cold fear as she came to the realization Finn was likely holding the key to the electronic pickpocket scheme in his hand.

"I need to hang onto this. Finn, you aren't in trouble, but you're being taken advantage of. Pizza Guy is using you and I think he's trying to make you commit a crime for him."

"He is too in trouble," Virgie squawked. "He's sitting here talking to strangers, taking their equipment, getting paid and then keeping it all a secret. You bet your britches he's in trouble."

"Ok, so you are in trouble. And I kind of agree with your grandma. When an adult tells you to keep something secret—especially when it's an adult you don't even know very well—that's bad. They are probably trying to keep themselves out of trouble."

Brandy looked at the device. "Did he show you how it works? How do you turn it on?"

Finn gave her the same brief tutorial Pizza Guy gave him, but she cautioned him not to actually push any of the buttons.

"So, did you actually use this yet? Did you download any data yet?"

"Not yet."

"Ok. Well, that's good at least. Do you think there is any way you could reverse-engineer this?"

"What does that mean?"

"Do you think you could learn to make one of these yourself by taking this one apart?"

"Yeah, probably. But what if I can't put it back together?"

"Don't worry about it. You're not going to get in trouble if you break it. I have an idea and I just want to know first if you can figure out exactly how it works. Because if you can, I think we can actually use this device to catch the thief in the act."

"What thief?" Finn asked.

"Someone has been stealing other people's credit cards and using them to buy stuff. It's against the law and I'm trying to find out who did it because my credit got stolen and I'm mad about it. I think the thief is using this machine to do it."

"Could I get a reward?" Finn asked.

"I'm sure you could." Brandy turned to Virgie. "Let him keep this one," she said, holding up the suspicious device. "We're going to catch a crook in his own cyber web."

CHAPTER TWENTY-FOUR

It was the call Brandy had been waiting for.

"Hello, Beautiful. I have some good news for you," Peter said.

"I'm nervous. What is it?"

"A certain Eric Jenkins is being booked into the city jail as we speak."

"Yessss!" Brandy hissed in victory as she pumped her fist in the air. "Did you get to talk to him? What did he say?"

"No. I didn't get to talk to him, but I talked to Randy, one of our detectives, and I was able to read the reports. You're not gonna believe this guy!"

"I bet I will," Brandy said sarcastically.

"So, first, he tried to blame Emily."

"Emily?" Brandy shrieked in surprise. "Why Emily?"

"Because she taunted him by taking his wallet— which, in his twisted opinion was the proximate cause of everything that came after. According to him, it was all her fault he got falsely accused of stealing your credit card so it was all her fault I had to question him and quote, 'embarrass him in front of his customers' by asking them to prove he was being honest. He got so worked up about it, he decided that if he was going to get accused of being a thief, he might as well live up to it and get something out of it in the process."

"Are you kidding me? He stole my credit just because he was mad about being accused of stealing my credit?"

"Yeah. That's what it boils down to."

"But how did you get roped into it? Why did he lie on that purchase agreement at Hyundai?"

"Ha ha," he laughed. "This is where it gets really good. He apparently had it in for me because I was the one who had the audacity to actually 'question his integrity.' Again, his twisted logic was that if I was going to question him—never mind that I'm a cop and it's my job—that he was going to call *my* integrity into question. It had nothing to do with you and me. Sounds like he would have done it to whatever cop knocked on his door and questioned him."

"He's crazier than I thought. I mean, I always knew he was kind of obsessive and once he got an idea in his mind, it would eat him up. He could never let things go, but this is next-level. Think of what he might have done if he knew we were dating."

"Well, he knows now because Randy point-blank asked him about it in the interview. I guess he blew up and then started trying to blame us for conspiring against him. He tried to suggest that he didn't do anything at the car dealership and that you must have known he got a new car and you were just bitter and jealous and planted the false purchase agreement or that you somehow know somebody at the dealership who did you a favor."

"What a nut!" Brandy marveled at the details as they unfolded.

"The evidence against him was overwhelming. He tried in vain for a while to throw you under the bus—insisting you were framing him because you have connections in the police department and the Chief will cover for you. He cited your 'attack' on his new girlfriend as proof that you're crazy. Which, by the way, kudos on the balloon bouquet. That was a nice touch."

"Thank you. But speaking of the Chief, I need your help with something."

"Of course. You need my help, or he does?"

"We both do."

"Alright, lay it on me."

"I have some good news of my own. I think I might have found the guy who's stealing everybody's credit cards."

"For real? How?"

"Well, I'm not sure, but I have a super-hot lead." Brandy told Peter about Finn and how he had been propositioned by the Pizza Guy who left a suspicious device in Finn's custody.

"I tried to look online to see what these skimmers actually look like, but they can be disguised as almost anything. They all look different. This one looks kind of like a cell phone or a modified graphing calculator."

"So, what are you going to do?"

"I asked Finn if he could reverse engineer it and figure out how it works. If he can, I want to set it up so that instead of scanning for cards, it will send a signal to the police department—and specifically to the Chief."

"And what do you need me to do?"

"I need you to help me make sure the Chief is in the right place at the right time to discover the device and make the arrest."

"Wow. Ok. Let me think about how we're going to do this."

"I think I've already got it figured out. If Finn can set-up the device—it's radio controlled—can't we somehow set it to scan for the police department's radio frequency? If so, we'll have it send a little S.O.S.-type alert to the Chief. He'll know the skimmer was activated. We can put GPS tracking on the device—heck, even Caroline can do that—and then all he has to do is track the device and—boom—make the arrest."

"So, the Chief won't totally be in the dark? He knows you're trying to catch this guy?"

"He doesn't know yet. I haven't told him. But, if he can be the one to actually intercept the device's signal and make the arrest, then you can make sure everybody knows it was the Chief who cracked the case. I need your help to make sure he's the one who gets credit—that nobody else at the department gets the signal or takes the call or whatever. It needs to be the Chief. He'll look like a hero and maybe people will stop talking about how he just sits at the bar all day if they know he's actually accomplishing something while he's there. They won't be pushing so hard to force him into retirement."

"I think we can do this, Brandy. Wow. I feel like an actual cop!" he laughed. "We're going to do some real police work."

"Well, don't get used to it. So far, I solve crime better than half the people in your police department. Maybe the Chief should put me on the payroll."

"You're our best-kept secret. When you're done catching electronic pickpockets, maybe we can ride around town and look for stolen bikes. I had the coolest ever bright blue Huffy Thunder Road BMX bike when I was a kid. It got stolen from the swimming pool. Maybe I could turn you loose on some cold cases and you could reunite me with 'The Blue Bullet.'"

"You named your bike?"

"Yeah. Doesn't every kid?"

"I never named my bike."

"Then I'm sorry you had such a horrible childhood."

"Haha," Brandy said sarcastically. "Maybe you should go work for the Milwaukee police so you could be a motorcycle cop and ride a Harley Davidson."

"Nah, they work too hard. I prefer hardly working."

"Don't I know it," she teased.

CHAPTER TWENTY-FIVE

Brandy and Peter and Finn worked together to organize a plan. Finn told Brandy that the Pizza Guy was going to be looking for his device at the end of the week. They invited Brownout into the fold to lend what little knowledge he had about radios to Finn and to help "think like a criminal" in order to avoid having the Pizza Guy detect their subterfuge before they could put their plan in place. Peter went to work figuring out how to manage the Chief communications at the department and how they might be able to tap into the department's radio frequency. Brandy acted as project manager—strategizing and trouble-shooting as issues arose and keeping everybody informed and on task.

Brownout surprised Brandy by knowing more about radio operations than she had given him credit for. He seemed a bit bumbling when he had shown Finn his "direct line to the President," but he actually made some important contributions to the effort and improved the overall plan.

"We're gonna need to use a fill to encrypt the frequency," Brownout said with a smug Barney Fife sniff.

"What's a 'fill?'" Finn asked.

"A fill is a little device that we attach to this skimmer. It's also called a 'key loader' because it actually loads cryptographic keys into the skimmer and prevents anyone from intercepting our frequency."

"But what is a 'fill?' What does it look like?" Finn wanted to know.

"Well, that depends. We need Brandy." Brownout waved her over from where she was visiting with customers at the opposite end of the bar.

"Do you need another drink, Brownout?"

"No. Well, yeah, if you're offering. But, that's not why I called you over. I need to talk to that policeman boyfriend of yours."

"Why do you need to talk to him?"

"To tell him me and you are getting married and to stay away from my girl."

"Oh, ok," Brandy said as she playfully rolled her eyes.

"I need him to get me the Chief's radio frequency."

"Is that something he can get? How would he even do that?"

"You let me and the little genius here worry about that. I know what I need. And I need to talk to your cop."

"Ok, if you say so." Brandy gave Brownout Peter's phone number after texting him to make sure he didn't mind and to let him know to expect Brownout's call.

Brandy eavesdropped as Brownout asked Peter to find out the Chief's radio frequency. Brownout had a police scanner at home and knew that the Chief's radio had multiple channels. He needed one that he could jam to all other radio traffic—thereby creating a direct line to the Chief.

Brownout and Peter traded phone calls for about an hour as Brownout coached Peter through how to gather the information he needed. Peter called dispatch and got the Chief's system I.D. because he learned the police department's radio channels could only receive signals through a password protected frequency—it's what allowed civilians to listen to a police scanner but prevented them from joining or disrupting the radio traffic.

"And make sure to get your own system I.D. because you're going to be my test case. I gotta make sure this works and I can't radio the Chief and say, 'test test. Is this thing on?'"

Once Peter called with both his and the Chief's system I.D.s, Brownout prescribed the next step.

"Looks like we're going to need a dongle."

Finn laughed hysterically at the word "dongle."

"Don't you say that word at school," Brownout joked. "Why are you still here? Did your mom forget about you?"

"No. She said I could stay longer because I'm helping. She's coming to get me in a little bit."

"Oh good. Now about that dongle . . ." Finn laughed again, and Brownout kept emphasizing the word for comedic effect.

"A dongle is a type of fill. You remember what a fill is?"

"Yes. It fills the radio with encryption."

"Very good! A-plus for you. A dongle is like a USB port. We plug it into this little skimmer and jam up all the frequencies then we unplug it and voila—we have a device that will do one thing and one thing only: radio the Chief."

"Can we try it?" Finn begged.

"Yep. But you gotta give me a minute. I have to run home to get the dongle."

Brownout told Finn to keep his seat warm for him and warned him that he better not finish his beer. Brownout yelled to Brandy not to take his drink and that he would be right back. She acknowledged him with a wave.

As Brownout was leaving the bar, Danny and Caroline were coming in.

Danny looked sheepish and Caroline looked like she was on the warpath. She may as well have dragged him in by his ear. She stopped Danny and held on tightly to his arm just inside the door as she addressed everyone in the bar.

Speaking in a loud voice she said, "Alright. By a show of hands, who all saw this man in here at any time today? Any time at all. Hands up."

She gestured dramatically to Danny as if he were on display or a prize to be won at auction. "This man right here. Who saw him in this bar today?"

Ralph and Big Joe raised their hands.

Caroline yanked Danny to where Ralph and Big Joe were sitting at the bar.

"What time was it when you saw him here?"

"Oh gosh, I don't know," Big Joe said as if he were thinking. "Maybe between 11 a.m. and 1 p.m. or so."

"Yeah," Ralph said. "It was over the lunch hour. He sat here with us for . . . what would you say, Joe? An hour? Hour and a half?"

"That sounds about right," Joe said. "What's the problem?"

"The problem is I never got an alert saying he was at 'Olive or Twist.' He mentioned that he came here over the lunch hour, but his tracker shows he was at work the whole time. Which leads me to believe he just left his phone at work while he went out and did who-knows-what!"

"Well, I don't know what to tell ya," Ralph said. "He was here."

"He either left his phone at work or he's lying when he says he came here. Are you just covering for him?"

"How could we cover for him?" Big Joe asked. "You just walked in here two seconds ago and mass-interrogated all of us. We haven't even had a chance to get our stories straight."

She raised her eyes and cocked her head in acknowledgment that he had a point.

"We're on your side, Caroline," Ralph said with a subtle wink to Danny. "If Danny thinks he can come in here and get us to lie for him, he's got another thing coming."

"I have an idea," Big Joe said, further helping to distract Caroline. "You give us your phone number. You can call or text us any time. We'll tell you if he's here or not. He'll never know you asked. You hear that, Danny? You gotta be on your best behavior around us. We're working for the other team."

Caroline gave Danny a smug and satisfied smile as she gave Ralph and Big Joe her number. "You can put that in your phones as 'Team Caroline.'"

Pleased with her new counter-intelligence recruits, she finally relaxed and sat on a bar stool near the end of the bar where Brandy was standing. Danny had his back to Caroline for a split-second—just long enough for him to mouth the words, "thank you" to Ralph and Big Joe, before Caroline could beckon for him to come sit next to her.

Caroline ordered a gin and tonic but when Danny tried to order a Casamigos neat, she considered his request and promptly rejected it.

"You're not drinking tequila tonight," she said.

"Why not?"

"Because you turn rude when you drink tequila."

"I do not. What are you talking about?"

"He'll have a Miller Lite," Caroline said to Brandy with a confident smile.

Danny's shoulders sunk as he rested his elbows on the bar.

Virgie, who had been quietly puttering around behind the bar offered a prediction.

"I can see how all this is going to go down. You're going to drive him away by being so overbearing. He really is going to cheat on you, but you'll have him so freaked out over the consequences, he'll just murder you, so he doesn't have to deal with your wrath."

"Virgie!" Brandy scolded. "He's not going to kill her or cheat on her. My God!"

"You need to watch 'Snapped,'" Virgie said.

"No, we don't," Brandy said.

"Isn't that the show where the woman always kills the man?" Caroline asked.

"Yep. That's the one."

"How do you know that?" Danny asked Caroline.

"Drink your beer," she said.

As Brandy sat down their drinks, Brownout made his triumphant return with the "dongle."

"Oh good, you're still here," he said to Finn. "And so's my beer!"

"Did you get it? Can we try it out?" Finn said excitedly.

"Yep." Brownout let Finn do the honors and coached him through how to insert the dongle into the skimmer and fill it with encryption.

"That's it? That's all we have to do?"

"Pretty much. Hold tight, we have to call Brandy's future ex-boyfriend."

"Haha," Brandy whined sarcastically. "You're not going to be my back-up plan if you insult my boyfriend, Brownout."

Brownout called Peter and told him to stand by for a test run of the modified skimmer. After a couple of tries, Peter confirmed it was working on his end. Finn and Brownout had cooperated to set the skimmer so that when the thief tried to punch the download button, instead of actually skimming for cards, it would send an alert to the desired radio frequency—in this case, Peter. Now that they knew their system worked, they could set it to contact the Chief.

They gave it a few more test signals before Peter called Brownout.

"It's a little rough around the edges. I think the reception is bad. Can it be affected by weather or where you're at in the building?" Peter asked.

"It can. I know cell reception is terrible in this bar. Probably affects radio waves the same way."

"See?" Ralph said to Caroline. "Your tracker probably just couldn't connect to the wi-fi. Or was your battery low? I have one of the video doorbells and it gets really finicky when the battery is low—sometimes it rings, sometimes it doesn't."

Caroline shrugged. She was over it and had already gotten what she needed: two more people willing to keep an eye on Danny. However, they all stopped to listen when they heard Brownout make an unusual offer over the phone.

"I can go outside and piss on the ground. That will get you some better reception."

Peter must have declined the offer because Brownout tried harder to sell him on it.

"If I go pee outside and then stick a grounding rod in the pee—I could unravel a coat hanger or see if Brandy has one of her plant hangers. Anyway, I just stick the grounding rod in the pee, and it makes a kind of antenna that will boost the power of the frequency."

Again, Peter tried to discourage him.

"Well, ok. If you change your mind, let me know. I'm about to finish this beer, so I'll wait a couple minutes to point Percy at the porcelain, just in case."

Soon Finn's mom came to pick him up. Finn agreed to leave Pizza Guy's device with Brownout because he still needed to install some kind of GPS tracker.

"Do you know how to do that Brownout, or do you need another assistant?" Brandy asked.

"Well, I could probably figure it out. Why, do you know how to attach a GPS?"

"No, but Caroline does," Brandy said, bringing Caroline into the conversation.

"What are you working on?" she asked.

Brandy filled her in on the status of their scheme and told her they needed to be able to track the location of the device—but that it couldn't alter the appearance or be obvious to the Pizza Guy that his device had been bugged.

"Oh, no problem," Caroline said. "Danny, hand me your shoe."

"What?" he said with surprise.

"Hand me your shoe," she said slowly as if she had to dumb it down for him. "Your left one."

Danny took off his shoe and gave it to Caroline. She took a nail file from her purse and used it almost like a knife blade to separate and open a small space between the sole and the arch of the shoe. She then used the tip of the nail file to fish a small silver disc out of the hole. It was about the size of a cell phone computer chip—smaller than a quarter.

"Here you go," she said as she handed the chip to Brandy. "You can use this one. But I need it back. You just stick it inside the skimmer. Meanwhile, I'll change the alerts so that instead of coming to me they come to you. Do you want them to come via text or email or both?"

"Um . . . text?" Brandy said, still a little surprised Caroline just happened to have a GPS tracker in Danny's shoe.

"You know, it's illegal in Wisconsin to track somebody with GPS without their knowledge or permission," Brandy said.

Caroline turned to Danny. "Danny, can I track you with GPS?" she asked dryly.

"Yeah," he said with a shrug.

"There, permission granted," Caroline said.

Ralph and Big Joe both gave Danny a look of sympathy because they knew he had no meaningful ability to protest or deny the "permission."

Meanwhile, Brownout popped the back off the skimmer and placed the GPS chip inside.

"Alright," he said. "I think we're good to go. And speaking of 'go' I need to either relieve myself or find a grounding rod."

Brandy pointed to the men's room and bellowed, "You're not finding a grounding rod!"

CHAPTER TWENTY-SIX

Next, Brandy had to inform the Chief that she was hot on the trail of the credit thief but needed his help to nab him and bring him down. Brandy did not explicitly explain that they had arranged for the skimmer device to connect directly to his radio signal or that he would be the only one notified when the thief tried to activate his device.

Instead, she let the Chief know that she thought the pizza guy was the culprit and that he was likely using a skimmer that looked like a simple hand-held credit card reader. She told the Chief she learned a skimmer would interfere with the Chief's radio. But she deduced the culprit would probably only skim for cards if he was in a crowd or in a situation where he could cast a wide net.

So, Brandy asked the Chief to order pizza for the department.

"Did Peter put you up to this? Sounds like a lot of work just to get a free lunch," the Chief joked.

"No. It wasn't Peter's idea. I wish I could give him credit—I wish the cops would have actually done something, but I did this all on my own. Well, not entirely on my own. Some friends at the bar who know how these electronics work helped me, but I think we're onto something. I order pizza at the bar all the time. He could have easily skimmed me and Big Joe at the bar. And that couple that you researched—you said they went to Red Box and the gas station and to pick up a pizza. At first, I didn't assume it had anything to do with the pizza. But after figuring out that their credit probably wasn't stolen at the Red Box or the gas station, it *had* to be the pizza place. Peter orders pizza at home—and his card stopped working. And—think about it—those pizza guys have access to every place in town. Nobody questions a pizza guy. They order pizza, the guy shows up, he takes their credit card. They never think about it again—until their credit is stolen. These guys have been hiding in plain sight. And now that I think I understand their scheme, I think you can actually catch them."

"So, what do I have to do?" the Chief asked.

"You order a bunch of pizzas so it will tip Pizza Guy off to the fact there will be a lot of people there to skim. When he delivers the pizza, you pay for it with a credit card. If he tries to skim your card with his card reader, you'll hear a signal on your shoulder radio—just a few beeps, like someone is trying to get your attention on that frequency. If you want to be extra sure—ask him to run the card again or to run a different card instead. If his skimmer is on, you'll get another alert and then—you arrest him right then and there."

"Ok, but is this one pizza guy or a whole ring of pizza guys? How do I know if I have the right guy? What if he claims he had no idea and somebody else just gave him that card reader to use?"

"Finn said the guy who gave him the skimmer is coming back for it at the end of the week. I'll order pizza every day if I have to until that same delivery man shows up. Then, I'll know he's working the deliveries and I'll give you the high-sign to call in your order. Then you can be sure it will be the same guy who owns the skimmer and told Finn to use it."

"So, all I have to do is wait for your signal, order a bunch of pizzas, pay with a credit card—or two—and, if I get an alert both times, arrest the guy."

"Yes. Exactly. I think this is really going to work."

"I'll do my best for you, Sweetheart."

"Thank you, Papí. I'll do my best for you, too."

"What does that mean?"

"I just mean, I'll do my best to help you nab the guy."

Brandy's plan was unfolding perfectly as the Chief began to independently entertain the idea of arresting the serial credit thief and looking like a hero. He fantasized about cuffing the guy in front of fifty hungry cops and rehearsed what he would say as he explained how he brought the culprit to justice.

He was also exceptionally proud of Brandy and wondered if his police work had rubbed off on her at all when she was a child and he brought her and Ginny on ride-alongs and let them turn on the siren. They weren't his daughters by nature, but he had nurtured them as if they were, and he couldn't help but feel a swell of pride that they had both taken an active interest in crime-fighting and solving mysteries—even if Ginny's were only imaginary and in books.

*   *   *

226

Brandy spent the next three days ordering pizza—it seemed they never sent the same delivery guy twice. She began to worry that perhaps he had somehow gotten wind of their trap and he would never come back to reclaim his skimmer device.

Meanwhile, everyone was sick of pizza. Even Hairy.

"I'm feeling lucky this time," Brandy said as she was on hold with "Pizza D'Action."

"Don't get any for me," Brownout said. "I'll just eat my sandwich."

"What's on your sandwich?" Brandy asked.

"Bologna and butter."

"Can I have it?" she asked.

"No. Get your own."

"Come on. I've eaten pizza every night this week."

"Same here. That's why I brought my sandwich."

"I'll give you a call drink for free," before he could even accept or reject her offer, Brandy started negotiating against herself. "I'll even do better than that. Chaz got a free bottle of Tom of Finland Vodka from the liquor distributor. He wanted me to save it for him, but I will even break open that bottle for you if you'll give me that sandwich."

"Bologna and butter knows no loyalty," Brownout said.

"Ugh!" Brandy said as she was taken off hold. She relayed yet another pizza delivery order and hung up the phone in disgust. "He better show up this time."

Brandy then texted the Chief and told him to be on standby—a little plan they had implemented in vain for the past three days. Still, the Chief was ready. As soon as he got the word from Brandy, he would place his own pizza order and put the bigger plan in motion.

And even though Virgie didn't usually work weeknights, she had been dutifully bringing Finn to the bar so that he would be there to hand over the Pizza Guy's device if and when he returned to pick it up. They would sit and visit with the regulars until the pizza came and then leave as soon as they were thwarted by an unidentified delivery guy.

Indeed, tonight was their lucky night. Finn's criminal mentor whipped open the side door and swooped in with a pizza a little after 7:00 p.m. Everyone quietly sprung into action or sat up at attention. Brandy hoped the shift in the atmosphere wasn't noticeable.

She tried to play it cool as she furiously texted the Chief. "It's him. It's him. He's here. Code Pizza." The Chief did not immediately respond, but Brandy trusted he knew what to do. Meanwhile, she pretended she needed to look for her purse as a pretense for giving Finn some alone time with the criminal.

"Here's your invention. Do you want it back now?" Finn asked when Brandy was in the back office.

"Sure. Did you get a lot of downloads?"

"I think so," Finn said with a shrug.

"Because if you did a good job, there's more in it for you. Maybe I could bring you a new one to test on Monday."

"Okay," Finn said, playing along.

Brandy returned with her purse and eleven dollars in cash. It pained her to pay him almost as much as it pained her to choke down another one of his stupid pizzas. He thanked her and gave Finn a friendly pat on the shoulder as he turned to leave.

"So, that's the guy?" Brownout said.

"I think so. We're about to find out. The Chief isn't responding to my texts. I hope he's getting them. Oh, I'm nervous. We have to pull this off!" Brandy said as she continued to tap at her phone.

Pizza Guy must have wasted no time trying to download his data because he hadn't been gone five minutes when he returned and approached Finn.

"Hey, kid, come here a second," he tried to show Finn to the door, ostensibly to go outside where he could talk to him in private, but "hey kid, come here a second" is the universal Call of the Kidnapper and when Virgie heard those words she sprang into action.

"Don't you go with him!" she yelled to Finn.

Finn stood frozen by his bar stool, not sure if he should go with the Pizza Guy in furtherance of the sting operation or not go with him in compliance with his grandma's orders.

"What do you want with an eleven-year-old boy?" Virgie said to the Pizza Guy.

"I just had a quick question for him."

"Then you ask it through me. There's no question a grown man has for an eleven-year-old boy that can't be said in front of all of us."

Virgie was ruining it. Brandy stood frozen like Finn, not sure if she should intervene or even how to insert herself. She couldn't suggest to Virgie of all people to just let Finn have a private side-bar with this potential kidnapper. But she also couldn't force Pizza Guy into a confrontation over the device and risk him realizing they were onto him.

Fortunately, Pizza Guy took the lead.

"I think your kid ripped me off," he said. Then turning to Finn, he addressed him directly. "Did you break this? Or drop it or anything? There's nothing on it."

"No," Finn said but Pizza Guy was growing impatient.

"Show me what you did." He handed Finn the device. "Show me exactly which buttons you pushed and how you downloaded things. I don't think you did it right."

Virgie stood-by supervising the test. She, of course, knew that Finn was embroiled in the sting, and would tolerate a discussion under her watchful eye, but no way was she letting that child out of her sight with a potential criminal.

She tried to play along, but again, only took the situation from bad to worse.

"Why are you having a child do your dirty work for you?" she asked.

Brandy gave her a hard stare, willing her to pipe down.

"It's something I invented. I just wanted him to test it out. It's not a big deal."

"Not a big deal?" Virgie squawked. "Ha! Then why don't you test it yourself?"

"An invention, huh? What's it do?" It was the Chief. He had come through the front door and quietly approached them from the side.

Brandy felt the plan falling apart. The Chief wasn't supposed to come to "Olive or Twist" and confront the guy! He was supposed to test him to make sure he was actually trying to skim cards by ordering pizzas and trying to pay with a credit card. She had set everything up so perfectly and now the Chief had gone rogue.

Pizza Guy stammered to explain his device to the Chief.

"It's, uh, it's like a digital wallet."

"Filled with other people's money?" the Chief asked.

"What do you mean?"

The Chief pulled out his wallet and took out three or four credit cards and store cards. He fanned them in front of Pizza Guy like a poker hand.

"Show us how your little device works," the Chief said.

"No," Pizza Guy said scanning the bar.

Virgie moved Finn behind her as Big Joe got up and stood next to the Chief.

The Pizza Guy was looking skittish.

"I said, show me how your little invention works."

"I don't think it will work in here," he lied as he tried to back up toward the side door.

The Chief advanced step by step for every backward move the Pizza Guy made and Big Joe inched forward alongside the Chief. Virgie braced Finn behind her and stepped forward. Brandy, sensing she might need to jump into the fray, took her tooth out and stared Pizza Guy down as she sat it on the edge of the cash register. The tension was palpable as Hairy gave a low warning growl.

With Pizza Guy nearly surrounded, Brownout said, "You don't want me to stand up."

"Show him your invention," Big Joe said.

With a shaking hand, he took one of the Chief's cards and held it to the device. The Chief's shoulder radio sprung to life with three quick beeps.

Pizza Guy then suddenly bolted toward the side door. But Hairy was blocking his path and started barking viciously. As Pizza Guy walked backward to avoid Hairy, the Chief grabbed him by his arm.

"You are under arrest."

"For what? I didn't do anything. This is entrapment!"

"Ha! Soliciting a child to use your skimming device for you and getting caught red-handed is entrapment? Did you know that enticing a child for criminal purposes is a felony? Matter of fact, a few other crimes come to mind: credit card theft, identity theft, fraud . . . the list goes on. You're going to have so many charges against you I'll just take my pick when we get to the jail. How does that sound?"

Pizza Guy tried to protest but realized he had been set up. "I told you not to tell anyone you little brat!" he said to Finn. "You owe me my twenty-dollars back!"

Hairy growled at the Pizza Guy as Finn climbed back up on his bar stool.

"Twenty dollars is the least of your worries," the Chief said as he called for patrol to transport the arrestee.

The bar erupted in applause. As the Chief was on his radio, Ralph staggered out of the men's room while everyone was still clapping and whooping. He stopped, took a bow and slurred, "I'd like to thank the academy . . . Oooh! The pizza's here!" He grabbed a slice and slumped back into his bar stool before adding, "I wouldn't go in there if I were you. I'd let that breathe for about an hour."

As the Chief took Pizza Guy outside to wait for his ride to the city detention center he ran into Emily--literally. She was coming in the door as the Chief and Pizza Guy were going out. Pizza Guy was handcuffed, and the Chief didn't want to give him any leeway, so the three of them did an awkward dance that made them look like they were playing a game of "Twister" in order to get through the door. Emily wove through and under the culprit's arms and around the Chief's middle before finally being spit through the human car wash into the bar.

"Did I miss everything?" she asked.

"Nah, I'm still as handsome as ever," Brownout said.

CHAPTER TWENTY-SEVEN

Early the next day, Peter called Brandy.

"Turn on the news," he said.

"I can't, I'm in my car on the way to work what's going on?"

"The Chief's giving a press conference."

"Are you serious? What's he saying?"

"He gave us the low-down at a meeting earlier this morning. He explained that he was part of a sting operation at 'Olive or Twist' and, with the help of some good-Samaritan civilians, had laid a trap for an electronic pickpocket ring that culminated in an arrest last night. And, by the way, there were a few more arrests, too."

"Fill me in. I haven't talked to the Chief at all since last night. What happened?"

"Well, some of this I got from our meeting and some I got from talking to Randy, one of our detectives. But, first, tell me what happened on your end, because I gather things didn't go down the way they were supposed to."

"Not exactly, but all's well that ends well. I thought the plan was for me to notify the Chief once I knew Finn's Pizza Guy was doing deliveries. He would order pizza for the department in order to forecast a potential crowd of victims and he would get proof as soon as Pizza Guy tried to swipe his card because it would send an alert to the Chief's radio. And that would be his cue to arrest the guy. But, yeah, that's not exactly what happened."

"Ok. Because I was waiting for my free pizza and never got it," Peter joked.

"So, what did you hear? I'm dying to talk to the Chief. Why did he just show up at the bar when I texted him? Why didn't he order the pizza like we planned?"

"I guess he got impatient. Because he told all of us this morning, he was part of a sting and that he had set a sophisticated trap by installing both a GPS and a radio fill into a transmitter being used to skim credit cards."

"Let me call you back, I'm going to call the Chief. I want to hear what he did—or what he thinks he did. Are you going to be able to talk if I call you back in a few minutes?"

"Sure."

Brandy ended her call with Peter and pulled to the curb in order to call the Chief. He answered on the first ring.

"Mija!" he exclaimed, calling her 'my daughter' in Spanish.

"Papí! What's going on? Fill me in. I just talked to Peter, and he said you were on TV!"

"Well, I was a little bit ago. I'll do an update in a couple hours. Who knew this would be such big news?"

"Ok, so start at the beginning. Why did you come to the bar last night? That wasn't the plan."

"Because almost as soon as you texted me to tell me he was there, I started getting alerts over my radio, so I knew he was trying to activate the device. So, I logged onto the GPS app and could see the device was still at the bar—so I figured, he was too. I tried to hurry over there to catch him in the act. Why wait? I figured I had him where I wanted him. There was too much risk to try to set up another front by ordering pizza for the department. Anybody could have interfered, but I knew everybody at the bar was in on it and wouldn't get in my way."

"In hindsight, I like that you arrested him at the bar—that way the people who were victimized like, me and Big Joe actually got to see you in action and got to see you haul him away."

"And I made sure to tell everybody that at the morning meeting. I let them know that I've been at 'Olive or Twist' helping set up the sting. Sure, I may have had a Modelo or two, but it was strictly business."

"I hope they realize what kind of hard work and genius it took for you to figure out how to be in the right place at the right time," Brandy said while secretly congratulating herself.

"That little boy is the real hero. We're lucky he told us about the device in the first place. He did the right thing. He deserves to be recognized."

"Finn's a good kid. I think he would never forget it if you acknowledged the role he played in helping you catch these guys."

"But now everybody is asking me how I did it. I got a call from the Milwaukee Police Department first thing this morning. Their best detective, a lady named Scotty Contreras, called me special just to ask for a consult so I can help her solve some similar crimes in Milwaukee."

236

"What are you going to tell her?" Brandy was slightly concerned that the Chief was now out of his league. After all, he understood almost nothing about the technology they had used to track and catch the criminal. He seemed to have had a vague understanding of how credit card skimmers worked, but she was curious how he was going to explain how this guy's skimmer magically radioed him and him alone.

"I'm going to tell her—get to know your victims. Listen to them. Understand them. You helped lead me to this guy because you were paying attention. And because you were mad. As law enforcement, we have to trust our victim's hunches and follow-up on their leads because no one wants to solve a case more than they do. No one has thought about it as much as they have. And maybe I get a bad rap for sitting in the bar all afternoon, but that's where I'm doing my most important police work. I'm listening. I'm getting to know the community on their level. They talk to me like a friend and not like a police officer. And that's when you get to really know what's going on in town."

"Do the guys at the department know that?"

"They do now if they didn't before. Just watch my press conference."

"I'll try to find it online as soon as I get to the bar."

"It's was on Channel 8—the one with that news anchor named Chip Lavender."

"Ok. I'll look it up as soon as I get there. I'm proud of you, Papí."

"Thank you, Mija. That's the only reward I ever need."

She ended the call, but before she could call Peter back, Ginny called her.

"Did you see Papí on the news?" Ginny asked.

"No, I just talked to him."

"Well, I was sitting here eating lunch with the TV on
. . ."

"You were eating lunch at 9:00 a.m.? What's wrong
with you?"

"What? I at breakfast, like, five hours ago. So, lunch
is next."

"Ok, whatever. As you were saying . . ."

"So, I'm just sitting there, eating lunch and the next
thing I know, Papí is on TV talking about how he nabbed that
crowd-hacking ring."

"It was a ring? Peter said something about how they
made more arrests last night, but we didn't get to finish
talking about it."

"Yeah, so I guess there was a whole bunch of them.
Sounds like half the people who worked at 'Pizza D'Action'
were in on it."

"So, Pizza Guy sold them up the river? I need to call
Peter back. He was starting to tell me the story, but then I
wanted to talk to Papí first. Let me call Peter back and then
I'll tell you what he says."

She ended the call with Ginny and, finally, she called
Peter.

"Ok, I've talked to the Chief and Ginny. She was
saying you guys arrested a bunch of Pizza Guys."

"Yeah. Finn's delivery guy sang like a bird and threw
all the rest of them under the bus. So, we've been busy at
intake all night booking them. I guess they had modified their
credit card readers to skim credit cards—some were the
radio-controlled kind, and some were actually hardwired in
the pizza restaurant. They were skimming cards all over
town. It's kind of embarrassing we didn't figure out they
were the common denominator sooner."

"What should be embarrassing is that you didn't figure it out at all. I did—with the help of an eleven-year-old kid. What happens if you guys have a murder or something? Do you just make the victim's family figure it out?"

"Oh, those we deal with. If a woman's dead, we just arrest the husband. If a man is dead, we arrest the wife. Case closed."

"Why am I afraid you aren't joking? What if the victim isn't married?"

"Then it's the boyfriend or girlfriend."

"Ok, what if they aren't in a relationship?"

"Then the butler did it. Every time."

"Yeesh. I'm afraid to know what kind of crimes go unsolved around here if you guys have 'cold case' bike thefts. Well, I'm pulling into the bar. I'll let you go. Looks like Chaz is here."

"Tell him 'wha's up bro' from me," Peter joked.

Brandy walked into the bar. The door was unlocked but all the lights were still off. She could hear noise coming from the back office and decided to quietly start her opening tasks before she had to start babysitting Chaz. The morning had already been eventful enough without having to deal with whatever acts and omissions he would leave for her to sort out.

She spent about twenty minutes loitering and had just watered the plants when she decided she couldn't avoid him any longer. Fortunately, Emily pulled up while Brandy was still outside.

"Hey, Girl. I thought I'd find you here. I've been trying to text you," Emily said.

"Sorry. My phone's inside and I've been out here fluffing up my flowers. Come inside. I'm just opening the place up."

They walked inside and Emily followed Brandy to the office. As they rounded the corner, they caught the tail-end of a knee-jerk reaction. Chaz had been sitting with his feet propped up on the desk watching something on the computer.

"Was that *The Bachelorette*?" Emily asked.

"No," Chaz said, with a grimace.

"Yes, it was!" Brandy teased. "Busted!"

"I wasn't watching *The Bachelorette*," Chaz insisted.

"Then flip the screen back up." As Brandy and Emily had come into the office, he quickly slammed the laptop shut and tried for a split-second to look nonchalant. Brandy was calling him out and kept chiding him.

"Come on, Chaz. Open it!"

"Yeah, open it!" Emily joined in.

He sheepishly lifted the top and hit the enter button. As the screen came to life, it was emblazoned with a still-streaming episode of *The Bachelorette*.

"It's ok, Chaz," Emily said. "We all have our little secrets. Want to know mine?"

"Sure," Chaz said, eager to shift the spotlight off of himself.

Emily pulled a wallet out of her purse and held it up in victory. "Anybody hungry for . . . pizza?"

"Emily, you didn't!" Brandy said in shock.

"He's going to jail. He's not going to need it."

PAPÍ'S PUNCH

This riff on a coconut margarita comes out of nowhere to get the job done—just like the Chief!

Ingredients:

1.5 oz Casamigos Blanco
.5 oz Malibu Rum
.75 oz Lime Juice
.75 Simple Syrup
2 dashes Australian Orange Bitters

Preparation:

To Build Cocktail:

Mix all ingredients in shaker with ice.
Strain into rocks glass over fresh ice.
Garnish with fresh lime. Salt optional.

Notes:

For an eye-catching garnish, try coquito nuts.

About the Author

ARCHER HAY is the pen name of brother and sister writing team, Jim Archuletta and Kelly Hay. Together they were born and raised in Ogallala, Nebraska and are now based in Milwaukee, Wisconsin.

Their backgrounds include being, among other things, an actor, lawyer, police officer, US Marine, evil poppet maker, and chanteuse. When the two are not writing, they are deep thinkers who spend hours on group texts tackling such issues as, "do you fold or crumple the toilet paper?" and trying to one-up each other with gifs.

In addition to writing the "Olive or Twist" Mystery Series, they are also authors of the "Badge Of" humorous crime series:

Book One: "Badge of the Bone Ritual"
Book Two: "Badge of the Phoenix"
Book Three: "Badge of the Desert Sage"
Book Four: "Badge of the Waxing Moon"

Acknowledgements

Archer Hay would like to thank and acknowledge our beta readers and ARC readers for their critical insights and encouragement. We would also like to thank our family and the many friends and colleagues who inspired and supported our writing.

Connect with us

If you enjoyed our book, please let others know! The greatest compliment you can give us is your confidence in our work and your eager anticipation of our forthcoming books!

You can also follow us on social media:

https://www.facebook.com/archerhay
https://twitter.com/archerhaybooks
https://www.instagram.com/archer.hay/

Sign up to receive our monthly newsletter full of updates, insider insights, and exclusive content:

https://www.archerhay.com/contact

Made in the USA
Lexington, KY
08 November 2019